WORTHY LIVES

WORTHY LIVES

HAWTHORN ACADEMY BOOK SIX

D.R. PERRY

THE WORTHY LIVESTEAM

Thanks to our Beta Readers

Rachel Beckford and Mary Morris

Thanks to our JIT Readers

Veronica Stephan-Miller, Rachel Beckford, and Kerry Mortimer

Editor
SkyHunter Editing Team

LMBPN Publishing
PMB 196, 2540 South Maryland Pkwy
Las Vegas, NV 89109

Version 1.00, August 2021
(Previously published as a part of the megabook *Hawthorn Academy: Year Two*)
ebook ISBN: 978-1-64971-959-1
Print ISBN: 978-1-64971-960-7

CHAPTER ONE

The next day felt like running to stand still. Lecture was an afterthought, but remembering that Dylan was behind on Luciano's topics helped me pay attention for his sake. I shared my notebook with him, focusing enough to take notes. Professor Luciano lectured about the 1920s in Salem.

Bootleggers, rumrunners, and other clandestine operations were part of the local shifter and faerie history, with portals to the Under being used to evade the authorities. Magi stuck to recording the extrahuman secret history. Vampires ministered to patients during the Spanish Flu. A Dr. Brown had saved the most lives during that pandemic.

A few names from liquor-smuggling sounded familiar. Coach Murray's family now owned the Lyceum. The Merlinis and Micellos also rang a bell, but I couldn't place them. I raised my hand.

"Are those last two families still around, Professor?"

"Yes." He nodded. "The Merlinis are more obscure, but the Micellos helped establish Gallows Hill. Bartholomew Micello and Corwin Merlini are on the extramural team from that school."

"Bar and Crow," Dylan murmured. "Huh."

We all tried to blow off steam in Creatives. Dylan went to his corner again with the guitar. He'd gotten good enough that his band had a chance of winning the talent show. I didn't have an inclination toward art, performance or otherwise, but maybe I could help in some other way.

Nobody could see the folks on stage without lights. I jotted a note to Professor Luciano in the notebook about running the lighting booth. Moments later he replied, saying he'd get me in touch with Penelope Andros, the staff member in charge of the stage tech crew.

In Gym, Logan blocked out cheer squad moves with Dorian. Hal took notes and gave critiques. The rest of us practiced Bishop's Row, including orb-conjuring drills. Coach Pickman flat out said she wanted Dylan, Faith, and me to make her proud of the school's team, and Bailey, who was still in our Gym group for some reason, didn't like it. She headed to the showers with her uniform on, sneakers and all.

"What's her problem?" Dorian leaned in the doorway to the gender-neutral section.

"I don't want to know." Faith shook her head.

"You used to be friends," I said.

"I'm still on good terms with Hailey." Faith sighed. "We grew apart, I guess."

The silence felt as awkward as a turtle on its back. I broke it, changing the subject.

"So Dorian, you've got something to tell me?" I put my hands on my hips, hoping he'd talk about what Blaine said he overheard, but he didn't. "What about Logan?"

"What about him?" Dorian raised an eyebrow.

"Did you ask him to the dance?" I tapped my foot.

"Oh my God, tell me you did." Faith put a hand to her cheek. "He's been crushing on you all year."

"I did." Dorian took a deep breath. "He said he'd think about it."

"What?" Faith asked, her head tilting in sync with Seth's. Her familiar seemed as confused as she was.

"I goofed. Asked Aliyah about the dance right in front of him and he ran off." Dorian winced. "Can't blame him."

"I don't know why." I shook my head. "Platonic city over here."

"Grace said I should."

"Honestly?" Faith rolled her eyes. "Follow *your* heart, not Grace's. Is she going with Azrael?"

"No. She hasn't decided yet."

"Huh." Faith narrowed her eyes, probably doing social math in her head. "I could have sworn she had the hots for Az."

"Maybe." I shook my head. "But Grace said she has to date for social reasons, not emotional ones."

"Been there, done that." Dorian pointed at his armpit. "I smell like last week's liverwurst-and-onion sandwich. Better wash up." He walked through the door to the gender-neutral showers.

Faith elbowed me. "We reek almost as much as that. It's shower time."

Bailey cowered in the tiled corner, wrapped in a soaked towel, hair plastered to her face, neck, and shoulders. Her eyes were wide, and she pointed at something hiding in the steam to my right.

"Monster!" Bailey cried. She cradled her waterlogged pigeon familiar, who cowered in the crook of her arm.

I conjured solar magic and looked where she pointed again, expecting to see a spider or insect, but it wasn't anything that benign. Ember reared up, hissing at Temperance's grundylow from my shoulder. It smiled gummily at the bird in Bailey's arms like a frog about to eat a fly.

Seth barked. Faith's nostrils flared.

"Coach Pickman!" I hollered, my hands glowing brighter. "Help!"

I heard the squeak of sneakers on tile, but by the time our coach turned the corner, the grundylow had squeezed himself down the drain.

What it was doing there and why it had terrorized Bailey was beyond me.

You said it—terror. That's the only reason Tempe Fairbanks does anything.

"It's safe, Overton." Coach Pickman clapped her hands. "On your feet."

"I c-can't, coach." She either shuddered or shivered, probably the latter since the water had finally run cold. "It was after Chip." Her familiar cooed, rubbing his head against her cheek. "And he can't even fly."

"Whatever it was, it's gone now. On your feet, Overton. Dry off, tend to your bird. The third-years need the gym in five minutes."

Bailey got up, still shivering. Coach Pickman walked with her to the changing area.

Faith growled as we showered. At first I thought it was Seth, her familiar, expressing her anger, but no. Faith Fairbanks rinsed her hair next to me, sounding like a hellhound.

"I wish I wasn't a Fairbanks anymore." She balled her hands into fists around the towel she'd used to dry tight enough that her knuckles were white. "They do shit like this."

"But why Bailey?" I shut my water off. "And why now?"

"I don't know, but I'm calling her on the carpet. Tonight."

"How can I help?"

"You can't. She's my sister, my responsibility. Maybe I can pin something on her that'll stick. If I don't, she'll only get worse."

"Okay, Faith. Should I tell Hal?"

"I'll do that, but it's Fairbanks territory." She sighed. "Like walking into Mordor. You can't simply walk in."

"At least we got through showering in peace." We got our regular clothes out of the lockers and dressed.

"Yeah. Safer in numbers around water right now." She froze. "Dorian's alone."

We hurried out of the locker room, calling for him.

"Coach Pickman told us what happened and to stick together." Hal stood at the doorway to the gender-neutral area. "I stayed with Dorian."

Faith and I breathed a sigh of relief, then headed into the gym, where Bailey waited with the coach. After hearing her story, the coach wanted us to come with them to the headmaster's office.

We made a formal report, but he said a grundylow's natural habitat included warm, humid places. Unless we could prove Temperance had sent him there with malicious intent, nothing would come of it.

In the lab, we boxed up our gadgets and brought them with our display and the report to the gym. Students hustled to set their tables up. The faculty had assigned our spots, so each project was easily visible. My group finished ahead of the others, but we still had our hurdles.

The delicate communication orbs had to go on stands, or they'd roll off the table. They were made of glass and not magically reinforced, so that was tricky. At least the tables didn't wobble. Once everything was set, I walked around to have a look at the other projects.

On the way, I glanced at a pair by the door. Blaine Harcourt spoke to Hal Hawkins, frowning at Blaine's phone. Blaine tucked the device away and handed Hal a card like the one he'd given me the day before. Blaine went to mingle with the faculty, and Hal left the gym entirely. I stopped at the nearest table.

Only Grace was there. The rest of her group wandered around, up to the same thing I was. She pointed them out, and we waved. I caught her up on my conversation with Blaine and asked about Hal.

"I don't know." She shrugged. "Ask Kitty when you get to their table. Maybe he said something to her. What's got you so curious?"

"Just an impulse to investigate the investigator." I sighed. "Blaine's smart, but he seems out of touch."

"That's a dragon-shifter thing." She nodded. "Why not talk to Dorian?"

"Good idea." I glanced at the cooler on her table. "What did he do for that?"

"It's only ice." Grace sighed. "Literally, that's all. Conjured the cold, but it works. Check it out.

Her group hadn't done as badly as I thought, considering all the arguing. But while the perpetual cooler looked good and worked well, the report on the board had a problem.

"Your pages are out of order."

"No way!" Grace made a little strangled sound. "Dylan and Dorian posted them."

"Here, let's fix it." I took the mixed-up pages down.

Together, we made short work of the problem. After that, we wished each other good luck, and I went on my way.

I spotted Lena hiding behind her group's board with her opossum. Out in front, Alex mumbled something, glancing behind the board at her. I almost walked by and left them to their whispered conversation. But Alex turned his head, and I saw a mark on his neck.

Maybe I shouldn't have cared. Most folks at Hawthorn expected him to have hickeys. He'd been a player before we'd accidentally dated last year, after all. But this looked like a bruise, and he was trying to hide it by popping his collar. That style had been out of fashion for ages. On closer inspection, his futile attempt to cover the mark with makeup was obvious.

"This is good work." I kept my tone neutral, jerking my thumb at the water wheel.

"So what?" He didn't glare as I'd expected. Instead, his eyes scanned the room behind me. "I didn't enchant it."

"The reports look nice. I like the headings, and that font was an awesome choice."

"I had nothing to do with that either."

"Was it Michelina?"

"How do you know her?" He narrowed his eyes, hands on his hips. He met my gaze, but only for a moment. It reminded me of an injured shark I'd seen this summer in the recovery tank at Boston Aquarium.

"Familiar Bonding." Lena peeked out at me, and I gave her a tiny wave. "I spent an entire month with her in there, remember?"

"Stay away from her from now on." The unfriendly expression remained on Alex's face, but his voice lowered to a near whisper. I couldn't figure out why, since Lena was close enough to hear it.

Who's he afraid of? And how can you get him to tell you?

"Are you okay?"

"Why are you talking to me again?" He moved his hands from his hips, crossing them over his chest.

"Everyone's fighting like shas and sphinxes lately. I thought a civil conversation couldn't hurt." I raised an eyebrow, giving him a choice he hadn't bothered offering me the year before. "I'll stop if you can't handle it."

"Get out of here already." He glanced at Lena like he was warning her. She nodded and hid behind the board again.

"All right. Take care of yourself." I walked away, not bothering to look back until I got to the next table over. Lena was entirely hidden from the front, even her feet since the tables all had cloths with skirts.

I didn't want to go over there again, so I just caught her eye, pointed at the project, and gave her a thumbs-up. She grinned. That made the confrontation with Alex worth the trouble.

I stood in front of Noah's table. Their project was a scrying bowl, but they'd gone further than the instructions required. With Noah's solar magic, that made sense. Instead of a crystal bowl with liquid inside, they'd made a liquid crystal screen. Noah's solar magic backlit it so images would show up. It displayed the street outside the Witch's Brew, which bustled with people walking in and out to get coffee during Salem's busiest month.

The images were a step up from black and white but had little in the way of accurate color depiction. It wasn't the type of thing to watch action movies on, but still amazing work for students.

"Wow, Noah. You guys rock."

"Thanks, Aliyah." He grinned. "But I think your orbs will beat our screen."

"How do you figure?"

"We made one device, and somehow you managed six. Three sets of people can communicate on- or off-campus. Or do a conference call. Not too shabby."

"Maybe we went overboard."

"I expected nothing less, with Izzy on your team." He grinned. "She's been overachieving since you two were in diapers."

"I heard Jonah's a lot like that." I grinned back. "He's academically threatening, according to her."

"He says the same thing." Noah shrugged. "I think they're about even."

"Can I tell her you said that?"

"I guess, if that will help her feel better." Noah blushed and studied his fingernails, which were a metallic shade of green. "But I'm biased. I happen to think very highly of Jonah."

"Oh?" I raised my eyebrow.

"You caught me." He looked at the project board instead of my face. "I have a tiny crush. No big deal."

"All right." I nodded, realizing that my brother minimizing anything this much meant it was colossal.

"See you at dinner?"

"Maybe."

"All right." I headed toward my table because the judges would be by soon. For a moment, when I turned, I could hardly believe my eyes.

The floor in the gym seemed to shimmer like someone had covered it with a sheet of glass.

Or water.

"Shut up, you." I put my hand over my mouth. When I blinked, the strange sheen had vanished. Fortunately, so had the Evil Inside Voice. I joined my team without further incident.

We greeted the adults who came by. As the dinner bell rang, we left them to the task of testing and judging our work.

CHAPTER TWO

I waited in line for my pumpernickel sandwich. I already had iced tea because I wasn't in the mood for beverage roulette. Since I had been one of the last people out of the gym, I peered into the crowded dining room, trying to decide where to sit.

One thing I'd never liked about middle school was the segregation into cliques. At Hawthorn, despite the bullying situation, we hadn't had that dynamic last year. Bailey had been the only one who got catty.

This year, it wasn't as easy. With Dylan and Dorian's rivalry, plus Grace spread thinner than too little butter on toast, we'd lost our cohesion. I glanced at the exit, wondering why I hadn't grabbed a dinner bag from Penelope's window.

But I didn't want to be alone. My family was close-knit, and it saddened me to think my friendships at Hawthorn hadn't followed the same pattern.

I wondered again if Bubbe had new information about Clementine, and if she'd tell me. She'd helped last year with Hal's condition, but this time the police were involved. Maybe she couldn't say much.

My order was up, so I put the plate with my sandwich, fries, and pickles on my tray. I decided to sit with Faith and Hal to ask about Blaine.

"He asked about my time in the infirmary." He moved broccoli around on his plate with the fork. "If I'd heard anything about Clementine. And yeah, I know you mentioned magiglobular anemia to him."

"Sorry." Ember snored on my shoulder.

"It's a good thing." Faith patted Seth, who'd poked his head out of her bag to peer at the drowsy dragonet. "Hal shouldn't be ashamed of his illness, and those Tinfoil Hat people are supposed to be geniuses."

"Right." Hal nodded. "Maybe they can help."

"So, what did you tell him?"

"Not much." He shook his head. "Information's locked down. Nurse Smith and Zeke don't talk about it, and Dad's a space magus, so he can hide records in places even I can't find them."

"I'm worried about someone else getting hurt." I sighed, remembering the marks on Alex's neck. Should I tell them?

Would they care? I doubt it. Don't bother.

I blinked, about to defy the Evil Inside Voice. Of course they'd care. Hal spoke up first, and if we weren't all magi at that table, I'd have suspected he was an empath.

"There *is* someone we ought to keep an eye on." Hal glanced at Faith.

"Right." She nodded. "Alex."

"Explain."

"He's the weakest link in Tempe's chain." Hal finally took a bite of broccoli, mostly because Nin kept nudging his fork hand toward it.

"I saw something at the gym." I told them about his odd behavior and the aura of fear around him. And the mark.

"It's worse than I thought." Faith crossed her arms over her chest, her voice quiet and her face pale. "Tonight can't come soon enough."

"I know we talked about this after Gym." Hal put his hand on her arm. "But you shouldn't go alone."

"I'm not bringing anyone." She shook her head. "Her familiar's a horror show, and I won't expose my friends to that kind of danger."

"What about Seth?" I put my hands in the table, leaning forward. "Aren't you worried about him? That grundylow's twice his size."

"I've got to bring him." She shook her head. "Without Seth, I don't have enough magic, not even after all the Bishop's Row practice."

"Ember, will you go with Seth? Be his wingwoman?"

"Peep!" She hopped down from my shoulder, landing on the table to pick her way carefully around the trays. When she reached the other side, she snaked her head under the table and peeped again. Seth answered with a bark and a wagging tail, his blue tongue lolling out of his mouth.

"Yeah, okay. She can come."

"That's better. What about Nin?" Hal asked.

"No." Faith covered Hal's hand with her own. "If it goes sideways, Ember can't carry both of them to safety."

"Do you know a psychic who can scry? I'd feel better with someone watching."

"I have a better idea." I grinned. "If Faith can wait until after the magipsychic fair."

"The communication orbs!" Faith smirked. "Genius!"

"Great. I'll smuggle a set out of the gym later."

We switched to cheerier topics, like the talent show in November and the December Dance. Hal's appetite returned, and he finished enough broccoli for Nin to stop squeaking at him.

Before we knew it, the dinner hour ended, and we headed back to the gym.

On returning to the gym, my stomach churned as if dinner was an entire glass of milk instead of a stomach-settling sandwich. The scene beyond the doors vindicated my rebellious gut immediately.

I'd imagined water all over the floor. Now a giant puddle stretched between the two rows of tables. How had it happened? Had the judges gotten in a fight? No. They had been in the cafeteria for the second half of dinner. The vandal had struck while the gym was empty.

"Our table!" I ran ahead, Faith on my heels. She'd seen the same thing.

The board wasn't damp, it was totally drenched. Ink on the posted report's pages had smudged and smeared, barely legible, but that wasn't all. We'd arranged the orbs in a circle, gleaming softly under the gym's lighting. Only three remained, and one had an enormous crack on its side. Purple-tinted shards littered the floor in front of the table.

"We've been sabotaged." Faith stood with her hands in fists, arms tight against her sides, nostrils flaring. Seth growled nonstop.

"Looks like it." Brianna stepped up beside me, peering at the remains of the orbs on the table. "There's no glamour. This was no changeling or faerie."

"This little mermaid says water magic." Cadence wrinkled her nose. "Ugh, it reeks like a bog."

"Temperance, or her little gremlin." Izzy's teeth squeaked as she ground them.

"It's a grundylow. Gremlins are kind of sweet, actually." I sighed.

"Pure faeries, not familiar material." Brianna nodded. "You really think they're sweet?"

"Nicer than the gnomes I've met," I answered.

"Don't geek out. This is a disaster." Faith glared down at the mess. "I'm getting the headmaster."

She stormed toward where he stood with his mouth wide open. I didn't have time to watch them talk or go listen. Instead, I grabbed a cardboard box and started collecting glass shards with Brianna and Izzy. Cadence refused to touch the water, so she rummaged through her backpack, looking for the rough draft of our report.

"Did anyone take any pictures?" Brianna asked.

I shook my head. "Mundane smartphones are pointless here. We're only allowed to call home in the office."

"Draconian much?" Brianna sighed. "Should've taken a Polaroid, but I was waiting to see if we won something. That won't happen now. Mom's going to cry."

"That sucks, Brianna. I'm sorry."

"Not to worry." We both turned to find Blaine Harcourt walking up behind us. "I took pictures of everything with LORA."

"Who's Laura?" Brianna asked.

"You mean, 'What's LORA,'" He corrected. "It's Kim's magipsychic app that tracks coincidence. I'll send you what I took. Brianna Collins, is it? From Gallows Hill?"

"Yeah, thanks."

"Don't thank me yet. At least one of your professors won't accept snapshots for the written portion. Aliyah needs a copy of your report." Blaine shook his head.

"But Professor Luciano's a good guy." I blinked.

"Are we both seriously talking about Filberto Luciano?" Blaine blinked. "He's an old friend of my mother's, who's not exactly a ray of sunshine. I'm grossly understating here."

"I've heard of Hertha Harcourt." I nodded. "But Luciano's been nothing but kind to me."

"He's got reasons." Blaine studied his fingernails.

"Which are?"

"That's his story to tell." Blaine gave us a golf wave. "I've got to rejoin the other judges. Good luck with old Filberto. I sincerely hope he doesn't make you rewrite your report."

"Maybe you should talk to him now." Brianna jerked her chin at the professor, who'd joined the conversation between the headmaster and Faith. "I'll get the rest of that glass."

"Thanks."

I walked toward them, but the group broke before I got there. Faith met me halfway.

"Are you okay?" She peered at me. "You look like you've seen a ghost."

"No ghosts, but Blaine said he thinks we'll have to rewrite our report."

"What? Why?"

"Apparently, he knows Professor Luciano."

"That's weird."

"Not so much." I shrugged. "Dragons never look the age they are."

"We can ask about the report later." Faith continued toward our wrecked project. "Let's group up before the judges hand out scores." She sighed, hanging her head. The noise she made was somewhere between a laugh and a sob.

"At least they saw it before. Hopefully, they remember it fondly." Azrael initiated a group hug in front of the table.

"I can't believe this happened. We worked so hard," Izzy moaned.

"I know." Cadence sounded like she'd lost a puppy. "This was the best I ever scienced in my entire life, and there's no proof."

"Two orbs still standing, Cadence." Azrael pointed. "That's proof, right?"

"About those orbs, guys." I winced. "I kind of need to borrow them later if that's okay?"

"I guess." Cadence sighed. "Easy come, easy go."

Headmaster Hawkins made his way around the room, pacing past each table. Before he got to us, Coach Pickman hurried over with a sponge but no bucket. Somehow, it absorbed all the water and sat more heavily in her hand.

"Maybe she's born with it, maybe it's magipsych," she muttered, walking toward the locker room with the sponge.

Finally, the headmaster stopped at our table. He sighed, shaking his head.

"This is an awful shame."

"When will we find out how this happened?" Cadence put a hand on her hip, tilting her head to deliver her best fish-eye. "Inquiring minds want to know."

"It might take us some time to answer that question."

"What happens to whoever did this?" Izzy raised an eyebrow. "Will they get expelled?"

"Yes, if it was intentional, but it's possible a familiar did this. In that case, we send the magus and their companion to Familiar Bonding."

"Well, okay." Izzy shrugged. "I guess not every critter is as well-behaved as Ember."

"Izzy, that was rude." I elbowed her. "And Ember's no angel. I trust Headmaster Hawkins to do the right thing."

"Thank you for your vote of confidence, Miss Morgenstern," he said, reaching into the large brown envelope tucked into the crook of his arm, "And I will present you with this." He pulled out a red ribbon and handed it to her.

"We won?" Cadence blinked. "But our project got ruined!"

"It wasn't ruined when we looked at it earlier, and one of the categories was teamwork, which the lot of you amply demonstrated."

"Wow." Brianna pinched herself. "The only time I ever won before was at sports."

"That's second place, Miss Collins." He gestured at another table. "Top honors go to Logan Pierce's group. Their group dynamic was, shall we say, more challenging than yours."

"Thanks, Headmaster." Faith smiled. "It's a relief after all this, you know." She waved a hand at the ruined project

"You're welcome, Miss Fairbanks." He glanced at the two remaining orbs. "You'll have to turn those over to Professor Luciano tomorrow morning. He's responsible for storing all the devices."

"Okay." I nodded, opening my bag and reaching for the orbs. He cleared his throat.

"Since communication orbs are not permitted in the dormitory, they must remain in the gym overnight."

"I understand." I tucked my hands behind my back, crossing my fingers.

In the end, I got help with the orb-smuggling operation. Grace's umbral magic made it almost too easy.

CHAPTER THREE

Dog's Night
Faith

I tied my hair back with the elastic Aliyah had lent me. She said it was lucky and I hoped it was true. I'd need that in spades.

"Come on, Seth. We've got work to do."

Placing the orb carefully in the bottom of a frilly oversized tote bag, I thanked the gods its styling hid the glass device inside. Seth went in with it, of course.

Hiding a forbidden activated communication orb with Hal and Aliyah listening at the other end was easy, and getting my sister alone wouldn't be difficult. Confronting her was like throwing rocks at a beehive when you had a severe sting allergy. I knew I'd have to be my own rescue medication someday, which was why I swam every night and busted my ass at Bishop's Row.

My parents sucked. They thought magi should rule the world, and they'd raised my sisters and me to climb the last few rungs of magi high society. They wanted nothing less than our family gaining more prestige than blue-blooded dragon shifters.

Charity was subtle and cautious, passing the buck and blame

whenever possible. For a while, they considered my directness refreshing, but that was before Temperance's first use of water magic in front of our parents. She'd sabotaged Charity's bonding process and scared the baby pricus off. Our sister ended up with a sand cat, which was below parental expectations. Then Temperance had turned around and bonded with Precious, her rare grundylow before I'd even met Seth.

So of course, Tempe became their favorite.

I discovered my blood relations weren't normal, let alone loving when I started at Hawthorn. Hal Hawkins had changed my entire life for the better, giving me a chance at a chosen family. I refused to let my sadistic sister screw that up.

In front of Tempe's room, I made the tightest fist I could and hammered the door. I shocked my knuckles on the solid wood, imagining myself an officer of the law come to bring justice.

"Who is it?"

"Faith. Open the door, Michelina."

Seth added a short, sharp bark, punctuating my request. She opened the door a crack, peering out so I only saw a forelock of mousy brown hair and one amber eye.

"*She* won't like that. What if she's angry? I don't want to be here for that."

"You could go to the library. Just let me in."

"Oh." She blinked, opening the door wider. "Hadn't thought of that."

"Thanks." I held the door, pointing at the pink-nosed critter behind her. "Take your opossum. I don't want either of you in range."

That distracted Lena long enough for Ember to fly into the room and perch on a rafter above the chandelier.

"In range of what?" She gathered the bundle of gray fur into her arms.

"Anything." I stepped aside to let her pass. "Earshot, line of sight, melee. You name it."

"Why?" She paused in the doorway.

"Because I know what she's been doing."

"How?" Lena's eyes widened. She turned, backing away from me into the hall.

"I have my ways." If Michelina wanted to believe I had omniscient psychic friends, I wouldn't contradict her. I had my own hunches anyway, and if I was lucky, Lena might say too much.

"She shouldn't have done it." Lena blinked. "I told her someone would find out."

"You were right. Now, skedaddle already." I waved my hands, shooing her into the hall. She scurried away.

I stepped in and closed the door firmly. Seth poked his nose out of the bag, pointing it at my sister's bed. I sauntered over, sat on it, wriggled a bit, and then reached under the mattress and pulled the hidden item out.

"Too predictable." I rolled my eyes at the journal.

Before I could open the book, it seemed to change shape and I dropped it.

It tumbled from my hands, my fingers suddenly slippery, as though it were made of ice. It bounced once, then vanished in the shadows under Lena's bed.

I peered under to confirm my earlier hunch and saw nothing but a dust bunny. It had to be a magipsychic device, though I couldn't be certain it was the one I most feared.

Temperance could have put together an extra toy on the side during Lab, but my sister couldn't enchant multi-element gadgets without friends, which she'd never make. All the same, I hoped the diary was a first-year-level charm. The alternative, that she'd smuggled a weapon used by war criminals onto our campus, was worse.

Behind me, she cleared her throat.

"The simplest explanation's probably true." I stood, turning the shoulder with the tote on it toward the wall behind me. "Hello, Tempe."

"So, you're not completely stupid. Maybe this won't be boring." My sister stepped out of her wardrobe, brushing a stray scarf off her shoulder. She tittered. "There. I'm out of the closet."

"You're straight, Tempe." Blunt instruments worked best on her.

"At least I'm not attracted to anemic little halfbreeds." She sneered.

"You're with Alex Onassis, and you criticize my taste in men?"

"Your beau won't make it to manhood. Hopefully, he dies before knocking you up and diluting our bloodline."

"Enough about boys. Let's talk about screwed-up magipsychic devices."

"I'm not done with *men* yet." She sniggered. "I'm using Alex, of course, but better than the way Grace used Dorian. He doesn't like how rough I play with him."

"That's abuse. The second I have proof, you're getting expelled."

"Proof of what? He's almost twice my size. Surely, if anyone's abused, it's me."

"You disgust me."

"Same." She laughed. "I hope you're grossed out by good old Grace, too. Power-coupling with a sissy is so last century."

"She dumped him. Copy that part."

"Alex must learn his place. I'll keep him, even though my real boyfriend is a way better smash."

"The imaginary studly boyfriend story again." I rolled my eyes. "Cut the crap. You heard me talking to Lena. I know what you did."

"You're bluffing."

"Prove it."

"I've got a pure element so I don't have to, but nobody trusts an undeath-dealing freak like you. Too bad Mommy didn't leave you in the bath as an infant."

She stepped forward, grinning, hands up. I knew what came next because she'd threatened me with drowning more times than I could count, so I held my hands up, palms out, fingers slightly curled the way Coach Pickman had taught us in Gym. And I conjured.

Seth whined in my bag, lending me strength as I pulled more undeath energy.

I wasn't sure it had worked, not until the water draped down six inches in front of me like a liquid sheet instead of over my nose and mouth. I'd never blocked her before and had spent years subjected to her whims, which generally consisted of "training" me to guard against her attacks.

Temperance only struck when something else hadn't gone her way.

It had felt strange, being an older sister afraid of the younger for so long. In books and movies, abuse came from bigger hands belonging to someone older. None of it looked like my experience, not until Aliyah told me about Alex. Maybe this battle wasn't just about Lena, the ruined project, or the poisoned familiar.

"What in Hades do you think you're doing, Faith?" Temperance snarled.

"Standing up." That was all I could muster through the strain of conjuring.

"I had no particular beef with you until tonight. Why bother?"

"Nobody deserves how you treat them, not even an ambitious twat like Alex."

"I already said I never hurt him." She batted her eyelids, her grin through the water reminding me of a corpse in a pond.

"Who bruised his neck, then? You can't lash out at me like at home, so he's your new scapegoat?"

"You're remembering things wrong." She snorted. "You're bigger than me. You must be crazy, accusing me of that."

"Bullshit." I struggled to take a breath. "I know what you are."

Seth whined again, trembling inside the bag. He was worried, and rightly so. All that talking had cracked my defense. Water splashed through, crashing against my shirt and drenching me from neck to toe.

I took a deep breath, focusing to conjure another orb. This time I spread my hands farther apart, hoping to protect more than just my face. I wouldn't put it past her to attack Seth. She'd almost killed him once.

"Get that mangy mutt, Precious." Temperance jerked a thumb at my familiar.

The grundylow crept out of her hair. She'd hid him in there since the day they bonded. I still couldn't believe she'd watched *Lord of the*

Rings and decided Precious was the perfect name for her familiar. And she called *me* a freak.

Any self-respecting magus or critter would dodge my energy. Grundylows had an affinity for both water and undeath, so he didn't care. Seth knew I couldn't hold both Temperance and her familiar off.

He leaped from the bag, glancing at the ceiling as he went. Seth was smart and knew I had to keep the orb intact. As fearful as he was at times, that sha was a fighter. He'd endured Tempe for years beside me, and this time, he had backup.

"Mount-Doom his slimy ass," I managed.

Our familiars circled each other, exchanging blows just once before Ember made her move. She swooped down, scooping Seth off the floor. Precious gibbered below, shaking one webbed fist at them. She alighted with him on top of Lena's wardrobe, where he sat growling down at the grundylow, whose hands were too slick to climb the varnished surface.

"You could just admit you're crazy and leave." Temperance glanced at the door and smiled at me. "I'd let you go."

"No. You're gonna stop."

"What? I did nothing wrong. You made Lena let you into *my* room and brought that flappy lizard inside."

"Everything. You'll stop now before anyone else gets hurt." I shook my head. "You can fool everyone else, but not me. I know what you're capable of. You're not allowed to terrorize this campus. I was here first."

"Charity was here first and gave *me* her blessing, not you. Because you're weak, freak." She snickered. "But for laughs, let's hear your deluded demands. Go on."

It amazed me how effortless it was for her, not lying but conjuring so much water. It exhausted me, defending myself and the truth, but I got a reprieve. She banished her water and put her hands in her pockets, tapping her foot like I was a joke. Or worse, an inconvenience.

"Dump Alex. Confess to wrecking the magipsych project, and don't mess with any living thing on this campus. That includes your roommate and all the familiars."

"He won't let me dump him, I had nothing to do with it, and I don't mess with people.

"Here's an example. You brought that illegal gadget in here, didn't you?"

"What gadget?" She snorted.

"The one from our basement."

"I never saw anything like that."

"You were with me when I found it."

"More delusions."

And just like that, I wasn't sure. It was years ago when we were in elementary school. Maybe I remembered it wrong, but I couldn't let Tempe use this tactic. I'd seen her skewer Charity with it.

I chose another weapon: decency on someone else's behalf.

"Lena's terrified of you. Stop scaring her."

"It's not my fault she's afraid to live with someone powerful."

"Our parents are loaded. Apply for a single. Leave her in peace, and break up with Alex. Smash your real boyfriend instead or whatever."

"If I dumped Alex, he'd kill himself." She giggled. I ignored how sick that was.

"You expect me to believe that?" I snorted. But if I was right and she had the device, she might be telling the truth. What if it did mind magic?

"He'll do anything I say." Her smile resembled a bleached skull. "Unlike the hot messes you keep around. They barely do things your way."

I couldn't take any more of my toxic sister. Charity had teased Aliyah last year because her uncle was evil. Tempe was at least as bad, maybe worse. If subtle, scheming Charity hadn't noticed, nobody else in my family would see it either.

"They're friends, not a Burger King franchise." I sneered. "Coincidence will catch up with you, and nobody will be on your side when it does."

"Get out of my room."

I raised my arms, and Ember swooped down to place Seth into them. She perched on my shoulder as I tucked him back into my bag.

In the doorway, I turned my head and looked over my shoulder at Tempe.

"Last chance. Cut the crap."

"I was right. You know nothing." She gave me a golf wave. "Talk, talk, least of my sisters."

She slammed the door behind me. Ember peeped on my shoulder, shifting her weight from one foot to the other. I didn't know much about dragonets, so I couldn't decipher her behavior, but Seth whimpered.

"What's wrong?" I got on the stairs and called out my floor, then checked on him.

His tongue lolled out of his mouth, its usual light blue color a darker shade. It looked swollen, too. He kept sticking it out, opening and closing his mouth, and his breath came fast and ragged, like chiffon shredding under a set of claws.

"I'll take care of you." I got off the stairs, prepared to head for Aliyah's room, but she was already in the hall, running like she knew I had an emergency. Because of the orb, I thought.

"Faith, we've got to get Seth to Bubbe's right now."

"Why?"

"Because I know those symptoms. He's been poisoned."

"It's past curfew, and the headmaster won't let us leave." I whispered, "And the orb, probation. You could get expelled."

"I don't care." Aliyah grabbed my hand, leading me toward the stairs. We got on for the first floor, but she kept walking, pulling me with her.

As we reached the hall that led to the street, Headmaster Hawkins appeared in front of us with a pop that would have startled me last year. Now I was used to space magic.

"Where are you going?"

"It's an emergency, Seth needs a vet right away."

"Let me see."

I held my familiar up for the headmaster. He took one look at my sha and opened the door for me, but he stopped Aliyah.

"Miss Morgenstern, you're staying on campus."

"Okay. Sorry, Faith. Remember, you're never alone."

I couldn't figure out why she'd said that or given in so easily until I remembered the orb in my bag. She and Hal would be with me all the way to her grandmother's. I hurried down Essex Street toward the extraveterinary office.

Doctor Morgenstern answered the door as I rang a second time. Her pastel-green hair stood up a little on one side. I'd almost forgotten about those random whimsical color choices. She held a cotton swab and a plastic vial in one hand.

"Did the headmaster tell you?"

"Yes." She rubbed the swab against Seth's muzzle, picking up some green foam, then put it in the vial. "Go straight back to the first room on the left."

I followed her orders immediately—a side effect of growing up in an unpredictably cruel family, I guess. I might have reacted quickly, regardless. Seth's life was on the line.

In the exam room, I set the bag on the table with Seth still inside. He'd been sick in there, and his fur was slippery with it. I turned, looking around for something to help get him out of the bag. Doctor Morgenstern had everything under control. She handed me a flannel blanket. I swaddled Seth and placed him on the table. He laid down on his side, panting heavily, more green foam around his mouth.

I stayed beside Seth, stroking his back, hoping these weren't his last moments. The doctor set the vial on the counter, the liquid inside turning purple. After washing her hands, she reached into a refrigerator under the counter, producing a syringe and a vial of medicine. Doctor Morgenstern unwrapped the syringe, stuck the needle in, and drew up a dose.

I watched, not nearly as fascinated as Aliyah might be. I used to consider medical practice squicky and bedside manner a display of weakness. My time with Hal as he managed his illness made me understand it took strength to seek help and to give it kindly. Everything good in my life would never have happened without Seth. Our bond was my first experience with love and care. I couldn't lose him now.

"Don't worry, Faith." Doctor Morgenstern put her hand on Seth's head behind his ear, which drooped instead of sitting straight up like usual. "It's the same poison that made Clementine sick, and this is the antidote. He'll make a full recovery, but I need you to hold him while I administer it."

I nodded, leaning over Seth and wrapping my arms around him. He kicked his feet, all four of them, struggling against the toxin. When the needle went in he whimpered, jerking a few times before lying still. I looked up at Doctor Morgenstern, sniffling.

"Is he okay?"

"Seth's okay. Listen to his breathing."

She was right. His body had stilled, but Seth's breathing had become even and measured, though slower than usual. He rolled his eye to meet my gaze and gave one more whimper, then wagged his long tail under the blanket. I kissed the top of his head. He licked my hand and closed his eyes. A series of snores made me hope he'd be okay.

"Thanks, Dr. Morgenstern."

"Any time."

"This is my fault." I stood, staring at my increasingly blurry hands. "I shouldn't have got into it with Tempe."

"Would you mind discussing that with me?"

"If it'd help Seth." I sniffled, embarrassed by the waterworks.

"I think so."

"Can I use your bathroom first?"

"Of course." She nodded. "I'll clean Seth up, make tea, and meet you in the kitchen."

"I'd rather have it here."

"Understood. I'll see you in a few minutes."

The little washroom was spartan and tidy. I'd gotten some of Seth's vomit and foam on me, so I washed my hands, arms, face, and even a section of my hair. Paper towels and soap took care of the spots on my shirt, which would go directly into the laundry as soon as I returned to campus.

But should I go back there? Shouldn't I insist on staying here? I knew Aliyah's grandma had a spare room, but I didn't want to ask for too much.

I headed back. Seth was clean, dry, and wrapped in a fresh blanket. She'd set up a folding table. The tea tray sat atop it, bearing a pot with a yellow cozy, two cups with saucers, and all the fixings.

I'd expected all of that, but not Doctor Morgenstern holding the communication orb. My bag was upside down in the exam room sink, still damp but dripping dry. That explained how she'd found it.

I froze in the doorway, wondering if she'd tell the headmaster. I'd get suspended, or worse, get Aliyah expelled.

"I thought it was bad, but not like this." She gazed at the device. Shapes moved across its surface, distorted from my side. I stepped beside her, trying to get a better look.

"That's my sister." I blinked. "But how?"

"Someone set it to record." She set it on the end of the table with Seth, who was nestled in extra blankets.

"Too bad it erases on replay. My Magipsych Fair group won second place with that orb. And I didn't toggle record." I glanced at the wall, lying to protect Hal and Aliyah. "I'm not sure who did."

"Seth's smart enough for that." She set the orb down in a nest of blankets. "You need to talk to someone, Faith."

"Tempe's the one who needs a shrink."

"She'll never admit that because she can't be honest. Do you know what gaslighting is?"

"Yes." I rolled my eyes. "Seriously, Doc. I'm seventeen, not seven."

"Nice sarcasm you've got there." She raised an eyebrow. "But this is serious. Temperance will continue making you doubt. That's why you need help."

"I don't need therapy."

"It's more than that." Dr. Morgenstern poured tea for herself, then held the pot over my cup and paused.

"Yes, please." I didn't want to have this conversation, but she'd saved Seth's life. The least I could do was listen.

"You need a record, corroborated by someone who believes you. I'm not talking about Hal either. Have you told him about Temperance?"

"I toned it down." I stared down at my tea, reluctant to sweeten it like maybe I didn't deserve it. "Didn't want to scare him away."

"You're standing by your boyfriend through a debilitating illness. Do you think a toxic family will scare him off?" She leaned back, holding her cup between tented fingers.

"Okay, you've got a point. But if his dad finds out, he might make us break up."

"Why do you think that?"

"Don't all parents keep the 'wrong sort' away from their kids?"

"There's no one way parents act. Most teach their children how to avoid harm, but yours didn't, and you don't seem to think they'll change. You need an adult to confide in."

"Headmaster Hawkins is the only therapist at school."

"Talk to me, then." She sipped tea. "I've got a license."

"If Mom and Dad find out I'm talking to a counselor—" I couldn't finish the sentence.

"Make appointments for Seth." She nodded in his direction. "He'll need regular checkups after this."

"Where'd the poison come from, anyway? I mean, you saw Seth tangle with Precious. Are grundylows poisonous all of a sudden?"

"No. All I can say is that this poison originates from a mountain town in northern Italy."

"Oh." I blinked. "Like Michelina. And Professor Luciano. Do you think they know each other?"

"Your sister's roommate?"

I nodded.

"I didn't know where she was from." She sighed. "My work on this case is limited by how much information the authorities give me, which isn't much. So thank you."

"My help backfires like I'm Hurricane Faith."

"I've felt like Hurricane Mildred before. Chaos is part of life. Feelings are always valid since they belong to you. How you act on them is your choice. I told Aliyah as much last year."

"Did it help her?"

"I'd like to think so, but I only give advice. It's up to the listener to take it or leave it."

"Can I bring Seth back on campus tonight?"

"He needs more care and observation. I discussed it with the headmaster when he told me you were coming."

"I don't want to leave him alone."

"I'll stay with him."

"That seems impossibly kind."

"Kindness is never impossible, but I think you know that."

"Maybe." I sniffled, the tears returning because she was right.

I made a second trip to the bathroom and washed my face, unashamed this time. Doctor Morgenstern acted like crying was the most natural thing in the world, and maybe it was.

She didn't want me walking home alone, so she called Aliyah's father down from upstairs, and he accompanied me back to campus. As I headed inside and up the stairs with the orb hidden in my still damp bag, I realized something.

My parents were wrong about practically everything, but I didn't have to follow in their footsteps. The most profound lesson for me at Hawthorn was rediscovering hope. It had become a dusty artifact locked away in the battered Seward chest in my mind.

Remembering where I came from was important, but understanding I could move beyond it was even more so.

It was after lights out when I knocked on Aliyah's door to give the orb back. She snuck out of the room with Grace, using Umbral magic to put it back in the gym. I didn't go, even though they offered. I'd had more than enough danger that night.

Back in my room, Kitty was already asleep with her sphinx curled up on the pillow beside her. I thought I'd have trouble sleeping without Seth, but exhaustion blessed me with thankfully dreamless sleep.

CHAPTER FOUR

Aliyah

I was relieved to see Faith return to campus, but not because of the orbs or even that utterly brutal fight with Tempe. It was all about how magi shared their lives with familiars.

When Ember's wing was injured, I'd been a mess, and I hadn't even officially bonded with her yet. I couldn't imagine how it was for Faith, who'd had Seth for years before school started. Grace understood that well.

"I'll check on her tomorrow before breakfast." Grace turned down her bed. "Are you in?"

"Absolutely." I helped a sleepy Ember off my shoulder.

"Was it Temperance? Who poisoned Clementine, I mean."

"I can't imagine how." I got in my bed. "But she had to be involved."

"How do you figure?" She kicked off her new slippers. Bunnies, of course. Lune shook his ears at them until Grace helped him up to the foot of her bed.

"Seth got poisoned in her room. Remember how Charity never got her hands dirty? Maybe Tempe's using a similar strategy. It fits Blaine's theory, too."

"Blaine Harcourt?" She sat.

"He thinks there's more than one person involved here." I filled Grace in on my conversation with Blaine in the library.

"That's messed up." She shook her head. "And yeah, she has access to other powers, but we can't do much to find out how. Faith shouldn't go this alone."

"So we help like you guys did last year when I went solar on the Bishop's Row court."

"Yeah. And last winter, how you stuck with me. You're a good friend."

"So are you, Grace."

"That's a topic for another time. Goodnight, Aliyah."

Before I dropped off to sleep, I said a small silent prayer that Seth would recover quickly.

The next morning, we waited outside Faith's room until she emerged for breakfast. We stuck to her like glue for the rest of the day. In Lecture, I sat in the middle row with her instead of in front. At lunch, Bubbe walked Seth in on a leash. She took it off his collar and he bounded straight to Faith, hopping into her lap to sniff her plate. She gave him some scraps, thanking Bubbe.

In Creatives, everybody talked about the talent show, which was the next extramural event. Over a month would go by since it happened after Thanksgiving, but that didn't dampen our excitement.

Dylan practiced the song he'd done with Noah at Sukkot, along with other songs by Fleetwood Mac, Noah's most recent retro music binge-fest. His skill improved every time I heard him play.

Grace sketched another entire set of outfits, slated for the crafts fair at the end of the year. She sat with Faith, asking her opinion on colors.

"It's a shame you can't make dresses on stage." Faith pointed at one design, a purple ombre suit with a peplum jacket and pencil skirt. "This one's super-sophisticated."

"What about a fashion show?" Logan asked.

"That's not a valid act for this contest." She sighed. "So what if I'm not performing anything? I'm busy enough."

"I'm doing everyone's makeup." Kitty grinned. "Maybe you can help in the dressing room or something."

"What about you, Aliyah?" Logan asked.

"The lights," I said, "Someone's got to make sure everyone sees you."

"Well, I won't be standing in them," Logan deadpanned. "I'm a recovering performance artist, remember?" He grinned as everyone laughed.

"More room for me then, my dude." Dorian peered at the sketch on Logan's easel. "I'm doing a standup routine."

"But you're not funny." Logan peered up, blinking slowly. Yeah, he was milking it, but we all laughed again anyway.

"You should really do the act with me, Logan, although I'm not sure I can call you a straight man."

My mouth dropped open. In all the drama over the Magicpsych Fair and Faith's misadventures, I had forgotten all about Dorian's plight with the December Dance.

"Are you guys going to the December Dance together?" Kitty clasped her hands together.

"If I'm lucky," Dorian replied.

"I don't know." Logan turned his easel, but not before I caught him blushing. "Still thinking about it."

Dorian moped, so Kitty left them alone about it. "What about you, Aliyah?"

"I'm going stag in a group."

"Sounds fun! Better tell Lee. He'd be all over that."

"He is. So's Izzy."

We all got back to our projects except for Dorian, who hung around nearby, pointedly not whittling the piece of wood he held.

"What's up, Dorian?"

"Do you think he'll forgive me?"

"I don't know."

"Well, can you put in a good word? I mean, you *are* his best friend."

That was interesting.

"He said that?"

"Says. All the time." Dorian sighed. "Please? I'd owe you big time."

"Maybe. Dorian, can you tell me what you overheard the day Clementine got poisoned?"

"Scaly Spice told me you might ask about that."

"Ha!" I put my hand over my mouth. "You seriously call him that?"

"Not to his face. Anyway, yeah. I'll talk to you about that day. In private."

"That's fine." I nodded. "Now, why not actually carve something?"

I showed Dorian the whittling tools, demonstrating what I'd learned while working on my misshapen figurine until the bell rang.

Lab was an uneventful observation of the botanical experiment from the day before. The tiny seedling hadn't grown much either, which meant tomorrow would be more of the same. I almost wished Professor Luciano hadn't taken it easy on us after the Magicpsych Fair, but I couldn't blame him. We'd all worked extremely hard and done excellent work, according to his comments on our reports.

During the rest of the week, Dylan haunted the café. He hung around the place way too much, considering he barely worked there anymore. Maybe he missed it, but every time I asked about it, he talked about the Lyceum instead.

Portia was still there, managing everything. Dylan said she was a total taskmistress, but it was good money. I asked if he'd seen Crow, but the bird shifter hadn't been to the restaurant during Dylan's shifts.

He never discussed the extramagus test, and neither did I. It hung unspoken between us like a floral wreath from a long-forgotten funeral service. Our conversations weren't easy anymore, though he'd dropped his grudge against Dorian. Neither of us seemed able to find the right words, and I wasn't even sure what I wanted him to know.

That you're into him, of course.

The Evil Inside Voice was right, but I couldn't say something like that. Dylan kept getting knocked down, like a small craft in a stormy sea. Confessing my feelings could be another wave, one that might capsize him.

The weeks stretched on like the now-bare branches reaching for gray November skies outside. There was a full Thanksgiving dinner being served on campus because of extramurals, but I invited all my friends to drop by my house for dessert if they wanted to.

On the holiday, Dylan, Logan, and Grace showed up. Izzy, Lee, and Cadence arrived after dinner at her house. When we finished dessert, the doorbell rang. Faith and Hal told us Kitty was up in New Hampshire at Eston's house. Dorian brought Cosmo over from the Hawthorne Hotel, where they'd had restaurant turkey with Blaine and Kim.

After sunset, Hailey walked in with Arick Magnuson on her arm. Bailey arrived with Brianna, Elanor, and Jonah, who gave Noah a big smile before sauntering into the living room.

You don't have to invite vampires in. The threshold thing was a myth. Besides the need to drink blood, which they could buy in cartons at stores and order in glasses at restaurants, they weren't much different from the rest of us.

Having so many visitors for dessert and coffee was nice. We even repeated last year's outing with Bubbe's babka and plastic mugs of hot chocolate, but this time, we hung around in the backyard, watching the boarded critters that were outside for exercise.

"I can't believe you grew up with all these magical animals."

Jonah had spoken to Noah. The two leaned together against the rail on our small back porch. The closeness of their hands mesmerized me. Was I about to learn some fundamental secret about how romance started?

Cadence elbowed me, then tilted her eyes to her right. I looked in that direction to see Dylan wearing a scowl, which wasn't remarkable lately, but Cadence rolled her eyes, tugging my sleeve and jerking her chin at the gate from the driveway. Her face fell like a rock off a cliff into the sea as Bar walked through and closed the gate behind him.

"What's wrong? Thought you'd be happy to see a friend from Gallows Hill."

She pouted. "He's just not the one I wanted to see."

"Why do you keep breaking up with Crow if you want him around?"

"He and I are too different, Aliyah." She shook her head. "You wouldn't understand."

"Maybe I do." I put my arm around my friend's shoulder, giving her a brief side hug before dropping it again. "But if you're not compatible, why bother?"

"I can't help it." She sighed. "There's just something about him, the way he walks. And how he smells. And that body. He usually hides it, but damn, he's sexy under that trench coat."

Troll changelings must have amazing hearing because Bar leaned against the fence beside the gate as though he'd been sucker-punched. He'd come over here on his own, probably to see Cadence, and found her obsessing about someone else.

That was something I understood, so I left Cadence chatting with Grace and got up to greet him. Maybe we could avoid the awkwardness of unrequited crush-clashes.

"Hey, how are you doing?" I held out my hand to Bar. "Welcome to my backyard."

"Thanks. Did you really know Cadence her whole life?"

"Almost. We met in kindergarten."

"Take a little walk with me?" Bar jerked his chin at the mulberry tree.

I nodded. We stopped by the enclosure, where some mercats frolicked in a small pond. Bar was massive, over six feet tall and built like a boulder. He leaned forward but not against the fence. I couldn't blame him. Cats with fishes' tails were mesmerizing, but the look in his eyes didn't match how I normally felt watching them.

"So, what's up?"

"This might sound weird, but the friend I usually talk to about this stuff has a serious conflict of interest." He took a deep breath and closed his eyes before continuing in a lower voice, "Do you think she likes grand gestures? When guys ask her out, I mean."

"Cadence?" I blinked. "She's a romantic, but not like that. She prefers making her own splashes. But Bar, I think you ought to know..."

"Yeah, I already do. She's got it bad for another guy. Conflict of interest, remember?"

"Oh." Bar's situation felt all too familiar. I wanted to help, but I couldn't even solve my own crush problems. "Well, does she know how you feel?"

"No. We don't talk about feelings. Usually, we just act."

"Why?"

He turned his head, and we stared into each other's eyes for seconds that felt like eons.

"I guess magi are different." He shook his head. "Trolls aren't big talkers."

"It's not much better for me. I can't tell the person I like, either. It's hard."

"Didn't used to be. Not until I started having so many more feelings, you know?"

"Maybe caring too much freezes people up like deer in headlights. It's okay if you don't agree, but I get it."

"Nah, you walk the walk. Must've been crazy, realizing you're an extramagus."

"It sucked. My friend's going through the same thing now, but I was lucky. It's been way harder for him. His family's overseas."

"Well, at least he's got you."

"I guess." Bar was right, but all I could think about was Hal saying Dylan didn't know I was alive. I changed the subject.

"Why don't you just ask Cadence to the dance? You've got to start somewhere, and technically, that's just one date."

"Yeah, I just don't know how to say it." He shook his head. "She's a mermaid."

"I don't either, and my crush is a magus like me." I glanced at Dylan, who'd taken out his guitar. As he strummed, Noah turned and started humming along.

"Oh, it's like that."

"Yup. Been that way for a while. I have a hard time with dating stuff."

"Hey, I got an idea."

"Oh?"

"Yeah. We count to three. I go ask her, you go ask him. Just say the first thing we think of."

"I would, but I told everyone I'm going stag in a group of friends. I don't want to let the people I already included down."

"That's easier." He grinned. "We ask them to do your friends thing?"

"You're pretty smart, Bar."

"Nah, just random genius flashes. So, what do you say?"

"Let's do it."

Cadence and Dylan both loved the idea, and Dylan said yes immediately. Cadence insisted we invite Crow. Bar nodded, so I agreed to it. It wasn't the ideal outcome, but better than nothing.

When we went back to school on Monday, we spent most of our time preparing for the talent show. There was a dress rehearsal, during which I discovered Alex was across the aisle from me in the sound booth. At least there'd be two walls and ten feet between us.

But there wasn't much time to worry about him. I worked hard, modifying lights in response to the shinier costumes. Everyone looked amazing, too. Grace had found an entire closet of forgotten costumes from Bubbe's school days and managed to alter them to fit everyone in record time.

I lingered in the cafeteria all through dinner, but Crow was conspicuously absent, along with Grace. I got a strange feeling in the pit of my stomach. Was this how Izzy felt when she had a premonition? Grace had never mentioned a date for the dance. I asked all our mutual friends, but they were clueless.

When I finally got the chance to ask, Grace said she hadn't decided yet.

CHAPTER FIVE

I read through some of Great Uncle Noah's letters in my free time. Almost all of them were love letters addressed to his boyfriend, a guy named Bert. They were cozily romantic, something I hadn't seen in fact or fiction before. My great uncle's love story was sweet and emotional, without any mention of sex. For some strange reason, it gave me hope that I might live my own someday.

I haunted the cafeteria and the lounge by the café, still trying to make good on my promise about Crow. Dorian dragged me away on Thursday night, insisting now was the time to tell his story. When I walked toward the empty academic wing, he paled.

"Anywhere but there."

"Okay." I steered him toward the stairs. "Why?"

"You'll know soon enough."

He knocked on his own door, which puzzled me at first, but when Eston emerged with Kitty, I understood. They giggled, and Eston's glasses were a little foggy.

"Hmm." Kitty glanced at us, then giggled again. "We have good timing."

"Oh yeah, we do." Eston grinned, pushing the door open wider and stepping into the hall so we could get through. "Have fun."

"Thanks." Dorian caught the door. "But we're studying, hardly fun."

The pair laughed, leaning on each other as they headed down the hall. Kitty looked back at my empty hands and called, "Don't forget your books, then!"

"It's not like that." I hung my head, hiding in my hair.

"Maybe we shouldn't go in there." Dorian sighed. "We don't want to start rumors."

"Too late. You already said we're studying, and this conversation is long overdue." I stepped across the threshold. "Anyway, you're courting Logan. Maybe they think this is for advice or a pep talk."

"Maybe."

He closed the door, waited for me to have a seat, and told me everything he'd overheard. When he finished, he sat. I got up and paced.

"So, there's good news and bad news, Dorian."

"Good first."

"We know who one of those people was."

"What's the bad news?"

"Confronting her won't work. She's a chronic liar, and you can't believe a word she says."

"Who is she?" Dorian shrugged. "I've got nothing."

"Temperance Fairbanks."

"How do you know?"

"Something she said to Faith about having a secret boyfriend, who she, um, likes better than Alex."

"That part fits." Dorian nodded. "And the guy wasn't Alex because everyone talked about how you fought in the lobby that day."

"It has to be a Bishop's Row player," I said. "Because of the point-set-match thing."

"Yeah, and a magus because of all the bigotry. So, how do we find him?"

"Process of elimination, and maybe a little research. He's a jock and he's straight, so it isn't Noah, but more than half the school tried out for our team. How do we narrow it down more without Tempe noticing?"

"Coach Pickman has me on filing duty because of my medical thing." Dorian grinned. "I could peek at the student files."

I stopped my pacing, turning to face him. He tugged on his collar and cleared his throat. Was he paler than usual? Bonier? More tired?

"You haven't mentioned that for a while. Are you okay? You look pale."

"Uh, it's only life-threatening without treatment. Basically, I have to wear, um, things that make it harder to do sports."

"That doesn't sound good. Can I help?"

"You already do every day." He let out a robotic-sounding laugh and tugged his collar again. "I'm only pale from skipping my veggies."

Go on. Ask again. Pry like he's an oyster.

I didn't. This was Dorian's circus and his monkeys. I'd give him the same respect I'd given Hal and let him talk about it when and if he wanted to.

"Thanks for the chat and the help, Dorian."

"Don't mention it. Literally." His shoulders eased. "And now I'm exhausted."

"See you tomorrow, then."

"Yeah. See you."

I left and headed toward my room to get ready for bed, refocusing my mind on finding Temperance's secret boyfriend. But I still said a prayer for Dorian Spanos, hoping he didn't have a debilitating condition like Hal's. He'd seen enough tragedy in his life.

I had the best seat in the house for the talent show, an unexpected benefit of the light booth. Everybody was amazing. I could hardly believe those were my friends and family. Yes, I said family because of Noah's band, Piercing Whispers.

The first act was Dorian's stand-up comedy. His routine lampooned ice, snow, and made popular culture references. I giggled through the entire thing, but not because the jokes were particularly innovative. Dorian had amazing comedic timing, and his delivery was spot on.

Next the curtain opened on Bar and Crow, dressed in garb that would fit right in at King Richard's Faire. Their stage combat routine had the audience gasping, whistling, and applauding. Bar threw glamour in there, but only to make sparks when their weapons clashed. I didn't know much about that particular performance art, but the routine made me want to give it a try.

After that came Izzy's and Jonah's ballroom dance routine. I expected a cha-cha, or maybe merengue, Izzy's favorite. Instead, they walked out dressed like Gomez and Morticia Adams and danced to *Vampire Club* by Voltaire, a Boston local musician who'd performed in Goth clubs and fan conventions since before I was born.

The fourth act was Piercing Whispers. I knew every one of the band's members. Elanor played keyboards and shared vocals with Noah, who played bass. Dylan rocked out on a brand new guitar in his favorite color, blue.

Where did he get the money for that? Even the Lyceum can't pay that well.

Behind them at the drum set sat the last person I expected. Arick Magnuson. His bookwyrm Skinner was coiled on his head like a beanie that bounced to the beat.

The other familiars all had some part in the performance. Gale swooped back and forth over the band, dropping glittering bits of ice. Elanor's phoenix FiFi backlit them. Noah's serpent Lotan sat atop Elanor's keyboard, swaying like a metronome. They played one of my favorite classic rock songs ever.

I'm talking about *The Chain* by Fleetwood Mac. Its music and lyrics had always hooked me because it reminded me of those moments right before disaster, like when a plate tilts against the edge of the table and you move to grab it. Will you catch it in time? Will it break to bits on the floor?

It had played in my room the summer before middle school when Cadence almost ran away from home. She came to me first, insisting I had to help her get to Boston Harbor. She planned to catch a transatlantic liner so she could jump off in open water and meet the undersea family her parents had left behind.

I called Izzy immediately and we'd talked her out of it, promising to stay friends forever. Since then, *The Chain* reminded me that our connections had real power. We could make a difference to the people in our lives and keep them from shattering on the floor just by loving them before they fell.

It doesn't make a difference to Dylan.

"I didn't ask you." I didn't have to suppress my outside voice alone inside the lighting booth.

Peace is practically a foreign country for you right now.

"This too shall pass. Along with you, hopefully."

You're arguing with me now?

"No, but maybe it's time we had a little chat." I brought the house lights up for intermission.

The moment this show is over, you'll be back in that mess with them. If I were you, I'd leave campus and never look back.

"I'm not leaving with a mystery poisoner on campus. You're just a voice in my head. What do you know?"

Plenty. And don't make assumptions about me or what I know.

I chewed on that, not daring to utter a response. If the voice's implication was true, it either had its own sentience or an origin outside my own mind. In the case of the former, a mental health crisis was imminent. In the latter, I'd been invaded by something incorporeal with an unknown agenda. Either way, I couldn't handle it on my own. How many of my friends had I sent to get professional help? Why couldn't I take my own advice?

You like having me around. I'm not all bad.

"Okay, fine. You're helpful sometimes. Broken clocks are right twice a day."

That's just incredibly rude. Perhaps I'll shut my figurative mouth indefinitely.

"Wait."

The voice made no response. Intermission had ended, so I dimmed the house lights. Backstage, the twins pulled the curtains, and I turned on the spotlight at center stage. Hal Hawkins wore a red satin tuxedo jacket with a white shirt and black tie. Faith stood behind him, smiling and waving, wearing a green and gold sequined gown slit to the knee. There was a box behind them on its side atop some sort of rolling frame. They began their magic show, not the extrahuman kind, but the illusionist type.

Hal and Faith had an entire routine where he did most of the prestidigitation and she assisted. Scarves flowed endlessly from one of his pockets and then her hair, and linked rings joined and separated. He even pulled Seth and Nin out of a hat.

Their finale involved the box, of course. Everyone expected him to make Faith disappear, and he did, for a moment. He opened the box the second time, but somehow they'd switched places, so she stood holding the lid while he climbed out of the box. After that, the pair bowed. I brought the lights down when the applause ended, which took a good bit of time. People had loved the twist ending.

I looked down at my list, seeing there was only one act left to go: Cadence, with a vocal performance. At the dress rehearsal, she hadn't played the music or revealed the title of her selection, just gotten up on the stage in a majorette outfit and done a mic check.

At first, I didn't recognize the opening bars of the music Elanor played. And yes, she was up there, a Hawthorn student providing backing music for one of the Gallows Hill students. We weren't supposed to collaborate since this was one event where the schools competed against each other, but that didn't matter because everyone forgot who was playing a moment later.

When Cadence opened her mouth, singing about how she can't make him stay, I understood immediately what she was doing: using *Famous Last Words* by My Chemical Romance to win the talent show and provoke her flaky ex-boyfriend, Crow. I saw him in the wings, jaw dropped and eyes wide.

When she finished, even I stood up and applauded. The power of her performance lifted me from my seat, an unseen force but absolutely real. Cadence's voice worked a bit like psychic empathy when she sang but was a rare magical mermaid gift that mimicked mind magic when spoken. I moved under my own power. A mermaid's singing voice worked by inspiring latent emotions into action, like the ultimate motivational speaker. She'd affected the entire audience because they all stood to cheer.

Other students joined Crow in the wings, and almost every one of them applauded. Bar stood there scratching his head. Changelings with strong enough glamour could resist Cadence's mojo. Something didn't sit well with him about her performance, but because I was affected, I had no idea what it was.

I kept the stage lights up, and the rest of the performers came back on the stage. The judges in the front row, who consisted of performers from town, stepped up on the apron and handed a score-card to Nurse Smith, who'd been the MC. He read each one, then held the tally sheet out in front of him.

"Third place, *The Chain* by Piercing Whisper." A round of applause from the audience broke out, strong enough to demonstrate our home-team enthusiasm.

"Second place, *Vampire Club* by Izzy and Jonah."

More applause followed, heavier this time. It subsided as everyone waited to hear who won.

"And the winner, *Famous Last Words* by Cadence."

Had the Gallows Hill kids used megaphones? When I opened the door to check, the crowd was so loud I had to cover my ears. I guess Cadence's performance was its own kind of magic.

Let's just hope no one accuses her of cheating.

"Thought you were shutting your mouth?"

"What's that?"

I stepped back into the booth, hands covering my mouth and eyes widening as I stared into Alex Onassis's face. The skin under his eyes looked puffy and dark like he hadn't slept well in weeks, and he wore a full face of makeup. I almost mistook the bruise on his left cheek-bone for a contouring effect. He stood in the doorway of my light booth, pulling a set of clunky noise-canceling headphones off. They weren't turned on.

"What are you doing here?"

"Running the sound." He rolled his eyes. "And overhearing you talk to yourself."

"Fine. But you hate me, so why are you here?" I gestured at the space between us.

"Everyone's still whammied like she said they'd be." He gestured at the headphones. "Except me. I don't have much time. Watch out for Temperance. She's planning something horrible."

"What is she going to do, Alex?"

He reached toward the breast pocket in his blazer where his basilisk usually stayed, but she wasn't there. His eyes widened for a moment, but he caught himself and smoothed his expression.

"She's been writing things down, stuff about where you and your friends go every day. Who's on what team, which competition. And all the upcoming events."

"How do we prepare?"

He opened his mouth, but it closed almost immediately after. When he tried again, his lips moved, but no sound came out.

"I *can't* say it." He bared his teeth, clenching his fists. "Dammit. Damn *her*."

His eyes widened and he stepped back, pressing his hand against his left ear and sagging against his booth's doorway. Had something hurt him? Nothing and no one was present in the room except us and Ember, who still slept. Unless, somewhere, someone was hurting his familiar.

"How did she do this to you?"

"I can't *say*." He sucked in a breath. "I can't do this. Shouldn't have done any of it." He straightened shakily, then staggered out of my light booth, slamming the door behind him.

I opened the door, intending to go after him, but by the time I did, the hallway was empty. I opened the sound booth and looked inside, but he wasn't there. When I went downstairs from the tech floor, the crowd was too thick. I'd lost him.

"What did he mean?" I asked Ember, who'd woken up and was peeping insistently in my ear.

She tugged my hair on my left side. I turned in that direction, only to find Temperance in the corner, grinning at me. Her grundylow peered out from behind her hair, eyes gleaming in the darkness.

She doesn't even have to touch that boy to harm him. I told you to leave campus.

In my head, I replied, *My friends need me. I'm not going anywhere. I can't save anyone by abandoning them.*

That girl's got the look of a killer. Act soon.

I hadn't feared her until that moment despite everything I heard Faith accuse her of over the orb, but now, Temperance Fairbanks terrified me.

CHAPTER SIX

I walked into the bathroom the night after the talent show. Faith swam laps in the pool, while Seth relaxed on a folded towel nearby. Ember glided down from my shoulder and sat beside him, curling her tail around her feet like a cat. I wasn't there to swim, so I stood where Faith could see me and waited.

At the end of her next lap, she crossed her arms on the edge of the pool and stared up at me.

"Is Temperance an extramagus? Specifically with mind magic?"

"That's a lead-pipe level of blunt." Faith shook water off her hand, then dragged it through her hair. "I don't think so. Her water came in early, but that's all I've seen her conjure."

"How early?" I put my hands on my hips. "Uncle Richard's fire came in grade school. Mom says he got water the year after that."

Faith sighed. "What gave you this idea?"

I paced along the side of the pool, telling her what had happened in the light booth and right afterward.

"Look, she's terrifying, but you can't go around accusing a Fairbanks of being an unregistered extramagus. My parents are horrible too."

"I don't want to poke the hornet's nest, but how else do you explain someone literally unable to talk like that?"

"Tell me again what Alex said."

"First he couldn't make a sound, and then it was 'I *can't* say it, I can't *say*' and he damned her. After that, he grabbed his ear and almost fell over."

"Yeah, that sounds like magic." She gripped the side of the pool, knuckles pale.

"And his familiar wasn't with him."

"That's why he doesn't dump her. If she's threatening his basilisk..." Faith slapped the water. "She's a monster."

"That explains a lot, but not everything. It looked like compulsion."

"I have one idea, but it's out there. We should check other possibilities first, like faerie stuff. A vow or something."

"I'll ask Cadence. She might not know, but she'll know who does." I sighed. "Sorry for ruining your swim, Faith."

"It's okay. It was important." Faith prepared to launch into a backstroke, but she stopped. "So's this. Tempe got her own room."

"How do you know?"

"Lena thanked me."

I gave her a grin. "You rescued her."

"Yeah, but I probably doomed Alex. When Temperance loses a victim, whoever's left suffers more."

I shivered. "I'm sorry. Enjoy the rest of your swim, and try to have a good night."

"You too."

I left the bathroom and went to find Cadence. She was in the fourth-floor hall, headed for the restroom with a bucket of toiletries. We went in together, and she took a minute to wash and dry her face. Afterward, Cadence glanced at me in the mirror while unscrewing a jar of moisturizer.

"What's up, Aliyah?"

"I have questions about glamour."

"I'm a mermaid, but I'll try to help. Go on."

"Can glamour work like mind magic? Make it so a person can't speak freely?"

"No, not at the changeling level. Not even most faeries. That's monarch-level stuff, like the queen and king."

"Oh."

"But Aliyah," she lowered her voice, "I've done it."

"Mind control?"

"It's a voice thing. I have to be direct—dot the Is and cross the Ts."

"How would Temperance Fairbanks manage it?"

"What?" Cadence stepped back, knocking her basket off the counter and spilling toiletries on the floor. "To whom?"

"Sorry." I bent down, retrieving tubes and brushes before they rolled away. "Alex Onassis."

"He's got big magic. You think she whammied someone that powerful?" Cadence bent over to help me. "Is she an extramagus?"

"Faith says no." I dropped the last tube of lip balm into the bucket. "So how could she manage it?"

We leaned against the counter, thinking. Finally, Cadence clapped her hands.

"What about a magipsychic device?"

"We're banned from bringing those on campus."

"That didn't stop you last year."

"Good point."

"I think you're looking for a gadget, Aliyah."

"Should I hit the library?"

"Are they open at this hour?"

"Yeah, all through December because of exams."

"So, let's go."

"Are you sure? I don't want to keep you from your beauty rest."

"I don't need it. I'm already gorgeous." She winked.

We headed out of the bathroom.

We weren't the first students in Hawthorn Academy history to hit the books in pajamas, but we were the only ones that night. The December Dance was on everyone's minds. I had a mystery to figure out.

I led Cadence to the giant index. Once we found listings on magipsychic gadgets, we ventured into the stacks. We took three volumes to a table and sat, flipping through them.

"What about this?" Cadence turned the book, tapping the illustration. "It blocks memories until people with trauma can work through them."

"I don't think it fits." I sighed, resting my chin on my hand. "He knew what he wanted to say, he just couldn't get the words out."

"What about something like this?" She flipped a handful of pages back to a different entry.

"Muffler?" I chewed my lower lip, scanning the item's description. "This turns the volume of voices down, either the user's or everyone around them. But it's a scarf, and he wasn't wearing one."

"I'm out of ideas from this book." Cadence shrugged. "What about that one?"

I opened another tome, turning to the index. We scanned the list, looking at the names and the brief descriptions of functions, but none of them fit.

"Is there anything I can help you find?" I looked up to see Mrs. Ashford, an infrequent helper in the library. She sat in a magipsychic assistive chair that glided above the floor.

"Yes, actually. You must know lots about this subject." I grinned. "We're looking for a particular type of magipsychic gadget, one that can do mind magic or ban a person from speaking on a certain topic."

"You won't find anything like that in these alternative therapies tomes." Mrs. Ashford sighed. "You want history books from the Second World War."

"Oh." Cadence blinked. "You think it's a banned device?"

"Likely banned worldwide if it channels compulsive magic. Those are nasty inventions, and they have a steep cost to use. Professor Luciano's doctoral theses are all on that subject. They're in collegiate libraries, unfortunately." Mrs. Ashford said. "The only advanced material we have is *A History of Axis Extrahumans*, and it's upstairs."

"Thanks, Mrs. Ashford."

"I'm a librarian, so it's my duty to keep you informed." She grinned, but it didn't touch her eyes this time. She wasn't old enough to have lived during World War II, but she must've heard stories from people who'd been there. Like Bubbe's dad.

Cadence and I brought the alternative therapies books to the desk, setting them in the return bin. *A History of Axis Extrahumans* was easy to find. We both yawned our heads off as I checked the book out.

Back in my room, I tried to read by the light of my solar magic, which Grace slept soundly through, but I fell asleep with my head pillowed on the pages.

I brought *A History of Axis Extrahumans* to class the next day. During Creatives, I flipped through it instead of working on art. Hal came to see what I was doing.

"Why are you researching Nazi magi?" he asked.

"To counter a bad apple." I mumbled Temperance's name while clearing my throat and Hal nodded. "They had some nasty gadgets back then. If only there was one that shut their effects down."

"Wait a minute." He scratched his head. "My Magicpsych Fair project was a switch, remember?"

"Yeah, but this is way more complicated than lights and bathtubs."

"Ooh!" Hal's eyes lit up. I'd almost forgotten how much he loved fixing things. "Tell me more."

"It's sensitive information."

"For my ears, or this location?"

"Location." I glanced around. "I'm trying to help someone unpopular."

"Okay." He reached for the book. "Let me see."

"I'm trying to see if one's being used on a person." I leaned my head on my hand. "And find something to stop it."

"Does this book have an index?"

I showed him. Hal speed-read the listings, with one finger under the words. Most were in German, with a handful in a less obvious language.

"I couldn't figure it out, so maybe you know. Why Greek?"

"Golden Dawn." Hal rolled his eyes. "Their magi helped the Axis back then."

"Ugh."

"I'm going to need a lexicon. Want to look it over during library time?"

"Sure." I looked him in the eye. "But only if you don't wear yourself out over this."

"I'm having a good day, so it should be fine. I promise to go straight to Nurse Smith if I start flagging."

"Okay, then."

We still had half an hour, so I got my clay container from the day before and sat with Lee, sharing tools to carve a brick pattern. I missed the cobblestone streets and brick architecture of Salem on this campus made of wood. Time passed quickly, but the design took shape under my hands until the bell rang. It went so well, maybe I'd have an entry for the Craft Expo in February.

I let Hal select a lexicon and retreated to a corner, settling into a tufted leather chair across from two more with a table between them. When Hal joined me, he had Faith in tow. I handed the book over.

"You and Cadence are smart. You two guessed my theory," Faith said. "I asked Tempe about a gadget. It was in my parents' basement five years ago, but it vanished the day after I asked her about it. She could have brought it here. If it's in this book, I'll recognize it."

I sat staring at her, but Hal's face went hard, eyes coldly bright like the day he'd discovered his illness. Hal Hawkins seemed mostly harmless, but his closest friends knew otherwise. He was prone to random bouts of righteous fury, and heaven wouldn't help whoever invoked it.

"We should call the FBE."

"We don't have proof." Faith sighed. "Calling them now is a boy-who-cried-wolf problem waiting to happen."

"Okay." Hal set the book on the table and opened it. "Let's see if anything looks familiar."

Faith studied each picture as we flipped through, searching in a more direct fashion than the night before. On page after page, she shook her head, but Hal stopped to peer at a gadget in a sidebar.

"This one's an Allied device, something they fought back with." He tapped the page. "It's constructed similarly to my project, but it nullifies magic when you flip the switch."

I wrote the page number in my notebook and we kept going. About two-thirds of the way through, Faith shuddered, wrapping her arms around herself.

"That's what I saw." She leaned forward to read without touching the page. "Says it stores all types of magic and drains energy when used."

"Whoa." My hand trembled when I moved to pat Faith's shoulder. "So, it hurts the person using it? That sounds counterproductive."

"It's not, though." Hal pointed at the text. "One Axis magus used it to firebomb a tank and chose to drain his entire platoon of mundane soldiers. They all died. No wonder it's banned."

"God." I put my hand over my mouth. I tried not to take the Almighty's name in vain, but this was horrifying. "How do we stop something like that?"

"What about that Allied nullifier?" Hal leaned his chin on his hand. "What do you think it'd do? Break Tempe's device?"

Faith grabbed my notebook and flipped the book to the page I'd marked down before.

"No." She read the description. "But see this? If she used it to ban someone from talking about her, it can shut that effect off."

"One-time use." Hal sighed. "Null magi can shut down any magic. Too bad there's none here."

"Well, can we modify your switch, Hal?"

"Maybe, but before I agree, I need to know." Hal looked at Faith, then me. "Who are you trying to save with this thing?"

The love of his life didn't tell him what she's up to? Oh, this is rich.

"You don't know?" I ignored the Evil Inside Voice.

"It's not Michelina Zanelli. I know she's out of the woods."

"Nobody deserves what he's going through," I confessed. "It's Alex."

His name hung in the air between us. Hal examined it, judging the worth of the magus who bore it.

"Yeah, he sucks." I sighed. "But we need more information. He tried to tell me, but he can't unless we fix his problem."

"I can't judge him for his screwy world view." Faith hung her head. "I'd be right there with him if it hadn't been for you, Hal."

"If you *both* agree the depressive demon nightmare boy needs rescuing, I can't argue." Hal nodded. "Let's do this."

We worked in silence for the rest of library time, checking every resource we could think of for information about nullification switches. We found a surprisingly comprehensive schematic in a magipsychic engineering manual referenced in the back of the first alternative therapies volume I'd flipped through with Cadence the night before.

Hal checked both books out and headed to Lab with the rest of us. I partnered with Dylan and Faith with Logan. Hal wanted us to give them a heads up in case we needed their help. Most gadgets required multiple contributors, and this one was no exception. Logan insisted on joining us, so we included him in the evening's plans.

Dylan, on the other hand, just nodded and changed the subject. I'd never seen him so focused on classwork. We'd moved on from recording the plant's growth to a perpetual motion device, so maybe that was it.

Why not ask about that new guitar?

I did.

"It's the Lyceum." He glued a blade on the fan at the top of the device. "One of the, uh, regulars is a fan, I guess, and she gave me an enormous tip the week before the talent show."

"Wow." I blinked. "She must really like you. Or something."

"I guess." The blade clattered to the bench. "A little help here?"

I didn't bother continuing that conversation.

After Lab, Hal stayed behind. Logan, Faith, and I waited in the hall, overhearing him ask Professor Luciano if he could bring his Magipsych Fair project back to his room.

"You'd like to do further study, is that it?" The professor raised an eyebrow, glancing at the doorway where we waited. "And you've got the time and energy?"

Faith turned her back on them, pretending to chat with me about my necklace.

"Yes. I'd like to explore alternate applications with some of my classmates. I think magical switches are fascinating. They have so many potential uses."

"That sounds brilliant, Harold. Of course I'll allow it." He sighed, reaching up to rub his temple. "But you must return it before winter break."

"I might want to work with it longer than that."

"Then you can request it again when the second semester begins."

"I understand, sir."

"Sir?" Professor Luciano gave Hal a worn grin. "You haven't called me that in ages, Mr. Hawkins."

The professor turned toward a closet and rummaged around for a moment, then produced a box labeled with Hal's name and exchanged it for a word of thanks. We met in the hall and walked toward the lobby.

Faith shrugged. "That was easy."

"Too easy." Hal glanced from one side of the hall to the other. "Do you get the impression something's not right with him?"

"He seems exhausted." I nodded. "And his familiar wasn't on his shoulder."

"Aren't exams stressful for professors?" Faith asked.

"Probably." I shrugged. "But he wasn't like this last year."

"Maybe he thinks we're doing the right thing." Hal hefted the box. "If he's got any idea."

"I wouldn't trust an adult advising against helping people, anyway." Faith rolled her eyes. "I'm glad he's our professor."

"Me too." I grinned.

Hal and Faith took the device up to his room while Logan and I went to Penelope's window to order four dinners to go. We'd work through the meal and have privacy. Lee was playing Truncheons and Flagons in Kitty's room that night.

I also stopped by the café to get pastries, teabags, and some apples for later. Logan helped me carry everything to the stairs. I called out our floor. Hal let us into the room, and I passed the food around.

"Thanks." Faith opened her dinner bag. "I'm starving."

We took a few minutes to eat because hangry studying wasn't productive. After that, we spread the books out on the floor, with the switch set out on a large piece of cardboard.

"I thought we were making a magic gadget?" Logan scratched his head. "That looks done."

"Modifying." Hal tapped the manual with the schematics. "We already have half the steps done if we start with this."

"So, it's like your project is the base unit?" Logan raised an eyebrow.

"Yeah." Hal nodded.

We finished the food and got to work, following the instructions. The manual restated that this device was for one-time use and would have to be recharged to nullify effects a second time.

"I'm not sure I'm comfortable with one shot." Faith brushed a lock of chestnut hair away from her face. "When Tempe retaliates, it'll be major-league."

"We have to work smarter," Hal urged. "Someone gets Alex alone before using it. She won't know how he broke out if we do that."

"But who?" I asked.

"Not you, Aliyah," Hal said. "You said he came to you twice. She'll be watching you."

"Wait." Logan looked up from the connection he just soldered. "Aren't you worried? I mean, it's Alex."

"Yeah." I nodded. "An agenda to escape. You didn't see him at the talent show, Logan. When he realized Asceco wasn't with him, he looked terrified."

"I'll do it," Hal said.

"No way." Faith shook her head. "You're about as stealthy as a bull in a china shop."

"Temperance will notice any of us," Logan said.

"Except Grace. Who can be invisible." I stood. "Should I get her?"

Everyone agreed, so I headed down the hall to fetch my roommate. Then I realized it was still dinner time, so she'd be in the dining hall. I was about to turn my back on the door to our room, but it opened.

"Hey." Azrael Ambersmith emerged, pausing halfway through.

"Hi." I blinked. "Is Grace in there?"

"Yeah." He leaned back, summoning her. I heard a muffled reply that she'd be there in a minute. He stepped all the way into the hall, closing the door behind him.

"Are you her date to the dance, Az?"

"No." He gazed at his shoes. "I just asked. She's going with someone else."

"Oh." It seemed pretty obvious to me that they liked each other. "Who?"

"You're not going to like it."

"What's up, Aliyah?" Grace came out of the room.

"I'm working on something with Logan, Hal, and Faith. We could use your help."

"Okay." She nodded, shutting the door. "Thanks for the glamour help, Az. See you later."

"Yeah, see you."

He went to the stairs and called for his floor. Grace insisted on fetching a smoothie for Hal to keep his strength up. I figured that was a good time to get the biggest sticking point out of the way.

"Look, we're doing this to help Alex, so if you've got a problem with that, I'll find someone else."

"Help him get away from Tempe?"

"Yeah."

"Count. Me. In." Her grin was so feral I almost jumped. "This is awesome." She ordered five pineapple smoothies.

"I didn't expect that response." I lowered my voice as we approached the crowded café. "He's your enemy, right?"

"He's been looking defanged lately. The enemy of my enemy is my frenemy."

"What's that?" I blinked.

"An It Girl mantra. It's catty, but I've got to do whatever works." Her smile didn't touch her eyes.

With the smoothies nestled in two trays, we ascended the stairs. At Hal's room, we walked in on a discussion about infusing the device.

"It's already got all the glamour and psychic energy it needs." Hal tapped the diagram. "Here and here, so we need to connect those parts to the barrel."

"What's it for?"

Everyone else drank their smoothies as I filled Grace in on the aftermath of the talent show. I included my conversations with Faith and Cadence afterward. She narrowed her eyes, then clenched her fists and paced in front of the door.

I let her be. That was how Grace put things together, and something had the wheels in her head turning on overdrive.

Faith and Logan made the physical connections as Hal instructed, but they called me over to help finish them with a little heat to reduce drying time.

Finally, Grace looked it over using the monocle Hal had in his toolkit, the one that let us see all the energies infused in the device.

"We need Cadence."

"We're trying to keep this as secret as possible." Faith shook her head. "And she's the biggest gossip on campus."

"Doesn't matter." Grace gave the monocle back to Hal. "Alex had no trouble talking to Aliyah until after Cadence sang in the show. I think Tempe put that power in her gadget somehow."

Grace handed the monocle over, and I peered through it.

"There aren't mind magi here, so she couldn't have gotten it that way, but what if she managed to meet one off-campus?"

"That is a theory question." Logan reached for the monocle and had a look. "A similar power can counter mind energy, like psychic empathy. Merfolk magic isn't well-documented, but Doris knows it. Cadence's voice ability is close enough."

"I get it." I nodded. "We only have one shot, but we can't risk her mentioning it because our entire plan hinges on Tempe not knowing how we're canceling her magic."

"There's only one way without telling her," Logan said. "Get her to do the mermaid voice thing in front of whoever's carrying the switch while it's hidden."

"But when?" I scratched my head.

"The dance." Faith answered. "She'll be totally distracted, trying to outdo Grace. And the sooner we do this, the better for Alex and us."

"The dance is tomorrow night." Hal sighed. "That crunches our time. We've still got loads to do."

"It'll go faster now that I'm here." Grace sat on the floor between Faith and Logan. "Crafting is my jam."

"I'm on self-care and rehydration duty." I opened the panel to the grooming station, fetched water, and heated it with solar magic to make tea.

The extra help did speed things up, though it was exhausting. Faith took Hal's hands during breaks, bolstering him with her undead energy. I passed food and drinks around like a waitress. When we ran out, I dropped by Kitty's to see if she had extra snacks at Truncheons and Flagons.

"We finished our dungeon crawl almost an hour ago." She handed me a bag of tortilla chips and a jar of salsa. "You guys are burning the midnight oil. Taking exams seriously?"

"I guess we are."

"Awesome." She peered under the round table. "Yes! Dorian left the rest of his Mountain Dew."

"Will he mind, do you think?"

"Nah. I'll tell him Logan needed it. Magic words." Kitty got a brown paper bag, plucked the salsa from my hand, and put it inside with the soda cans. She added a half-full bag of mandarin oranges. "Oh, and Faith donated these to my game, so I'm just giving them back."

"Thanks, Kitty."

Since it was Friday, we still had another hour to work. Our familiars had all zonked out during the last snack break. Hal switched from hands-on conjuring to reading the manual and supervising. Fortunately, the extra food helped us keep going, which we needed. The dance was in less than twenty-four hours at that point. It felt almost anticlimactic when we finished fifty minutes later.

We all yawned our heads off as we said goodnight only minutes before lights out. I was asleep before my head hit the pillow, while Grace sat up in bed, reading about Tempe's device in *A History of Axis Extrahumans*. She'd polished off the Mountain Dew.

CHAPTER SEVEN

I sat at breakfast with Hal, Faith, Grace, and Logan. All of our famil-iars dozed in the critter-friendly area in the corner. Grace was the only one without bleary eyes. I had no idea where her energy came from. She didn't even have a cup of coffee like the rest of us. Logan's arm stretched halfway across the table, supporting his head. He blinked wearily at me.

"I can't believe we built the whole thing," he mumbled.

"Modified, technically." Hal leaned against the wall inside the booth, using his hand as a pillow.

"Will it work, do you think?" Grace raised an eyebrow.

"Yeah." Faith rubbed her eyes. "If you shoot your shot at the right time."

"Thanks, guys." I yawned, stretching an arm overhead like I wanted a nonexistent teacher's attention. At second glance, I realized teachers were in the cafeteria. Professor Luciano sat in the corner with Mess-ing's Dean Adelphi over a pot of tea.

"That's what friends are for." Logan grinned.

"I didn't do much, but I'm glad I'm not the only one willing to help our old enemy."

"He doesn't deserve it." Grace shrugged. "And we need to maintain our winning streak."

"Yeah." Faith nodded. "She won't stop, but it'll be hard for her, losing an asset."

"Don't you care what happens to Alex after all this?"

"Not really," Hal said. "He took major advantage of you last year, Aliyah. Don't expect that snake to change his stripes."

Did you really think all their intentions mirrored your own?

I shook my head, putting three heaping spoonfuls of sugar into my coffee and stirring. I didn't care about their reasons, which weren't as informed as mine. I was the only one who'd seen the look on Alex's face that night.

His sense of helpless distress in the light booth had been pitiful, and he was unable to escape on his own. I couldn't save the guy I cared for, so I'd help the one I used to be with instead.

He didn't ask for help.

"Tzedakah is the greatest mitzvah." I blinked and put my hand over my mouth. "Oops."

"That's not a thing from Passover, is it?" Grace sipped her orange juice.

"No, but it's been on my mind since Yom Kippur." I wrapped cold fingers around my warm cup. "We've been so focused on winning everything, I worry I'll forget that helping is important."

They didn't freeze in place, but everyone got quiet and still. And stared at me.

"That'll never happen," Logan said.

"Yeah." Faith snorted. "That's like saying a fish forgot to swim."

"Or the sun forgot to rise," Grace added.

"As long as you don't let your guard down." Hal tilted his head, reminding me of his dad. "You can help Alex, but don't go trusting him afterward."

"No worries." I sipped my blissfully hot coffee. "He'll probably turn his nose up in the air and call me a do-gooder."

"Oooh, big insults." Grace made a duck face and waggled her fingers at me. "Aliyah, the Good Witch of the South."

"Salem's in the north." Logan scratched his head.

"Sorry." Grace winked, amping up her accent. "It's southern to me, don't you know."

Everybody laughed.

"Hey," Faith said. "Wasn't there a null magus in the papers a few years back?"

"Yeah." I nodded, then took a big slug of coffee. It was the perfect temperature, warm enough that it comforted my throat but cool enough to not burn. "Al Dunstable. He saved his faerie girlfriend from iron poisoning by canceling her troll magic. Nixed his Sidhe variety, too. Now they're regular magi."

Hal sat bolt upright in his seat, staring with eyes like twin moons. Faith put her arm around him. My sleep-deprived brain couldn't imagine why.

"Sounds interesting." Logan leaned over his coffee and inhaled deeply. "Tell it while I fall asleep? Like a bedtime story?"

"Yeah, tell us," Faith said.

"I think I'll doze off before getting a sentence out." I nodded. "I've got everything I know about it in a scrapbook at home. We can go over it another time."

They nodded, still leaning together with their arms around each other. Moments passed. Logan nodded a few times, then shook exhaustion off long enough to remember his coffee. Finally, it occurred to me why the story of Al Dunstable and Gemma Tolland would hit super close to home for Hal and Faith, and maybe even give them hope.

"How will you guys get through the dance?" Grace broke the silence.

"With a good long nap," Hal said.

"Why are you drinking all this then?" Grace pointed at the coffee.

"Because we don't have whatever you're using to look so chipper." Faith pointed at Grace's face, with its distinct lack of circles under the eyes. Then I realized how she did it.

"It's Umbral magic. She's as tired as we are, just hides it better. Am I right?"

"You got me." Grace smiled and tapped her nose. "I'm wearing this enhancement for an errand. After that, it's dreamland for a few hours."

"Beauty sleep," Logan said. "I need that."

We all had a laugh, then finished our beverages and breakfast. When we got up to bus our table, a snarky voice called out behind us.

"Look at the pajama crew. Field trip to Walmart later?" I turned to find Dylan.

"What?" I blinked, staring at my friend.

"You heard me. Looks like you spent all night with books, but there's nothing to study for right now. What were you up to, anyway?" He crossed his arms over his chest and raised his eyebrow.

"We'll talk later, Dylan." I approached him but he shook his head, glaring at me.

"Not now, Aliyah." He addressed me but glared at Grace. "I don't have the energy for your psychobabble."

Logan and Hal blinked blearily at Dylan and Faith rubbed her chin, but Grace slipped her arm through mine and led us all toward the dishwashing window.

"Don't mind him." Grace shook her head, sighing. "He probably just needs more time."

"No, Grace." I turned my head, staring at her. "He's had plenty of that. Plus time working on his music and hanging out with friends in his band. He's waiting for something. Maybe an apology?"

"It's been almost six months since we broke up. And what do I need to apologize for?"

"I don't know." I shrugged. "He's been through more than you think, what with discovering he's an extramagus."

"Look, I get it. It hurts to break up." Grace sighed. "But I had nothing to do with the extramagus thing. His attitude's gotten ridiculous."

"It's worse than you think for him. I can't say more than that."

"Why?" She shook her head. "Look, maybe you're a sanity unicorn. What if Dylan's just normal for an extramagus and having a mental break?"

I froze, stung as if she'd just slapped me in the face. Logan dropped his coffee spoon. Hal blinked.

"Holy shit, Grace, I can't believe you said that." Faith rounded on her, putting her hands on her hips.

"It didn't sound good." Hal shook his head.

"I'm sorry." Grace pressed both hands to her chest.

"Save it for Dylan." My face flushed, or at least it felt hot. Maybe it was my hand, channeling solar magic. I took three deep breaths before continuing, "Just two words. I'm. Sorry. That's it. Why is that so hard for you to understand?"

"Because I owned my issues last year, and part of that was refusing to take the blame for stuff that's not my fault."

"How about I give you a reading, Grace?" None of us had noticed Izzy approach, which made sense considering how tired we were.

"I don't believe in those."

"For amusement then." She shrugged. "Maybe it'll be relaxing."

The rest of us stared like we were at a CW drama-watch party.

"If the rest of you get off my case, fine."

"If you don't mind, I need to hit the hay." Hal shuffled toward the critter area, looking for Nin. "Before I have to hit the infirmary."

"The rest of you go back to sleep," Izzy said. "You all look like something the mercat dragged in."

We left, sleepily waving goodbye. On the way out, I glanced at Professor Luciano. Had he noticed Dylan's disdain and our subsequent argument? No. He hadn't gone to Dean Adelphi for social time. Cards covered the table between them, the tea pushed to the side. He was getting a reading, and at the center of it all sat the Tower.

Ouch.

Death wasn't the worst card to get in a tarot reading by itself. Two made it scarier: the Tower and the Chariot reversed. I glanced at the other cards surrounding the Tower. Mostly, they were cups and swords and not too bad. But there was the Chariot reversed in a future position, and Death was beside it.

The Professor didn't glance up, even though I'd been staring for a while. Dean Adelphi did, and she narrowed her eyes. I didn't wait around to see what she'd do next.

That reading was foretelling a catastrophe.

After seeing that, it should have been harder to rest, but I was almost asleep when Grace came in and went directly to bed. If we didn't sleep now, carrying out a covert plan to hoodwink Temperance at the dance would get dangerous.

I wore my dress from Parents' Night. It was amazing looking and comfortable, plus I didn't mind wearing the same special-event dress twice. Grace chose something completely different. It was a lavender and gold chiffon confection that draped across her body with no discernible fastenings, and it had a neckline that plunged to her solar plexus. Her footwear seemed risky.

At first, I wasn't sure why she'd picked six-inch platforms. I wondered how she'd dance in them. Kitty and Faith came by our room to get ready, joined by Cadence and Izzy later. The hour before the dance consisted of a flurry of preening, plus a few panicked moments where Cadence helped Grace struggle with dress tape.

Grabbing a handful of spare dress tape strips, I took advantage of her distraction. Grace's handbag sat on her bed, out of her view, so I headed toward it with the tape. Faith saw what I was doing immediately.

"Hey Cadence, if your voice isn't too tired, I'd love to hear another song." Faith stepped up to the mirror beside Grace with her eyeshadow palette and started applying.

"Okay."

Instead of a showstopping vocal showcase, Cadence regaled us with a sedate rendition of an old song her mother loved: *Tiny Dancer* by Elton John. I turned Grace's bag so it pointed at Cadence, opened it, and stuffed the wardrobe malfunction fixers inside.

Cadence had her back to the switch, but the space between it and her was unobstructed, a direct line of sight. I stood by the bag, keeping it open as long as I could. As she reached the end of the last verse, I closed it and went about the business of applying lipstick.

Let's hope it's enough.

A knock at the door made us all freeze in our tracks. At that point, we weren't expecting anyone. I went to answer it, hand glowing faintly because I worried it was Temperance. She'd been too quiet, and our wins against her so far suddenly felt too easy. I needn't have worried.

Logan stood outside the door, hanging his head and blushing.

"Hey, Aliyah? Can I go in your group of friends to the dance?"

"Of course." I nodded, banishing my magic. "You told Dorian no, huh?"

"Yeah, guess I chickened out." He sighed. "But I said he can ask me to dance once we're there."

"Do you want to talk about it?" I stepped into the hall, closing the door behind me and lowering my voice.

"I don't know." Logan tilted his head, peering at my face without meeting my eyes as if he expected to find something there he didn't like, but the tightness in his expression eased and the blush faded.

"It's all good if you don't."

"No, I should get it off my chest." Logan leaned against the wall, staring across the hall instead of looking at me. He had an easier time if he didn't have to make eye contact. "This is gonna sound stupid, but the way he asked, well, it felt almost insulting."

"Definitely not stupid. And I agree." One corner of my mouth tilted up. "Someone gave me advice that might also work for you. Here goes." I cleared my throat. "Your someone special should worship the ground you walk on and make you feel happy."

"My brain knows that." He sighed, gazing down the hall toward Dorian's room. "But my heart's another story. It feels like nobody understands what it's like."

"I absolutely do." I leaned close beside him, whispering, "I've had a crush on Dylan for a year and a half."

Logan's lower lip trembled as if he might cry. My breath caught in my throat, which choked up with tears I refused to allow to ruin my makeup. So I turned and reached out, and we ended up in a shaky sort of bear hug.

We'd done that before multiple times a day when he'd stayed in the room at Bubbe's office. This time, something was different. Not emotionally or in any weird hormonal way; physically, something was wrong. I glanced down briefly, then at his face again.

"You need to go back to your room before the dance, Logan." I loosened my grip, holding him at arm's length.

"Why?"

"Pants. You've still got pajama bottoms on."

"Oh!" His face turned red, like the first day we'd met. Logan's social gaffes and mistakes had diminished since then, at least around his friends. "Yeah, I'd better fix that. See you soon, Aliyah."

"Yeah, see you."

I headed back into the room and told everyone Logan would join us. Grace looked away, collecting her bag. We left minutes after that. Everyone else was ready, and the dance was about to start.

I stood in the third-floor hallway, waiting for the folks I'd invited to go in this group. Faith had gone to get Hal, and they showed up with Kitty and Eston. That made sense because they were on dates.

The rest arrived one by one, except for Izzy, who arrived with Lee, of course. Bar and Brianna showed up, Crow at their heels. Cadence smiled, and I was in the middle of a relieved sigh until the bird shifter headed for Grace. She passed her bag, nullifying switch and all, to me.

"It's up to you to save the prince of darkness," she murmured and stepped forward.

That was when I noticed his distinctively designed suit, complete with lavender vest and tie. Crow cleaned up extremely well, to the point where casting directors at Lifetime or the Hallmark Channel might clamor to give him romantic leads in teen movies. They linked arms.

Everyone's favorite it girl is about to make some unexpected waves.

"Grace?" I put a hand on her free arm, stopping her. "Are you seriously doing this?"

"Sorry." She looked me in the eye, at least. The regret there shocked me into letting her go. "I'm countering something. You'll see when we get downstairs."

She let Crow call out the first floor to the staircase. Hal and Faith followed them, along with Kitty and Eston. Their movements revealed Dorian, who'd been standing behind them. He stared and blinked, watching the stairs carry them away. After that, he hurried to my side.

"Aliyah, I've got to tell you something." His eyes were wide. "I just found out."

"Listen, we've got to go, or we'll be late." I sighed.

"But it's about—"

"We're going. Now." Cadence's voice cut through Dorian's like a knife.

We all followed her, although I wanted to wait for Dylan. It was as if her voice had moved my body. I could have resisted if I hadn't been so shocked by Grace and exhausted from the night before, but maybe I wouldn't have. Cadence was one of my best friends, and I'd never seen her this hurt. She needed me.

I stepped off the first floor too late to kick off the dancing as I had at all the other dances here. Music already played *I'm With You* by Avril Lavigne. As expected, Grace was out there with Crow, Hal with Faith, and Kitty with Eston. Noah had paired up with Jonah. Elanor stepped up to our group and asked Brianna to dance.

I looked around for Dylan, intending to drag him out there, but Logan put a hand on my arm and pointed past the other couples on the floor. My heart nearly stopped.

"No."

Dylan was out there already, dancing with Temperance Fairbanks.

I shook out of Logan's grip and hurried away, turning my back on the dance floor. I couldn't watch this. Thankfully, there were plenty of chairs in the corner. I headed toward them, but a voice I couldn't divorce from authority stopped me.

"Miss Morgenstern, may I have this dance?"

"Professor Luciano?" I glanced over my shoulder, and sure enough, he stood there, elbow out. I blinked.

Izzy stood behind him, between Lee and Cadence, holding a tarot card: the King of Cups. She nodded and I trusted her, but I still had doubts. A professor couldn't rescue me from a broken heart.

Perhaps he's got wisdom to impart.

I nodded and took his arm, wondering why the Evil Inside Voice reassured me. Mostly it expected the worst from everyone. Had it always been sympathetic toward my professor? A few gasps and whispers followed us, but they cut out at a word from Cadence.

"Professor, what's this about?"

"This." He pulled the lapel on his jacket, revealing a faintly yellowed letter in the pocket, with a familiar return address: 10-1/2 Hawthorne Street.

"Oh." I blinked. "But my great uncle's letters are in my room. I've been reading them."

"This is one of their counterparts."

"You're Bert?"

"Filberto. I only allowed Noah the elder to call me that." He nodded. "And you, just this once."

"Why are you telling me now?"

"It will come up in the near future." He sighed. "Inevitable events, I'm afraid."

"What do you mean? What's going to happen?"

"Further investigation." He sighed. "Due to the fear and turmoil on this campus. But you're an extramagus, in tune with more magic than your fellows. You can feel it if you focus." We reached the edge of the dance floor, so he spun me to turn us around.

I let him lead, and we locked gazes. He blinked slowly as though waiting for me to do something.

"How?"

"Close your eyes and clear your mind. Consider well what comes unbidden to it."

I tried, worried I'd trip or bump into someone. Making it through this dance without incident was important, but so was discovering the effects of all the drama this semester. All I could think of was Dylan and how he'd been that morning. Had Temperance gotten her hooks into him right after that? Or much sooner?

If I had any money, I'd wager his new guitar.

"Keep practicing, and it will come through eventually. I believe you've got the basic idea."

"How do you know?"

"Finish reading all the letters." He risked a fragile grin. "Your great uncle and I had much in common. Your worries aren't unfounded."

"How bad do you think it'll get?"

"I'm not sure. I believe you're stuck in a coincidental pattern, along with some of your cohorts."

"So, you're telling me to be on guard?"

"And prepared. Practice the exercise you attempted today each morning or every night. Perhaps both is best." The song ended, and he escorted me off the dance floor.

"Thanks, Professor."

"Thank me by continuing your studies and vigilance." He bowed.

"I will." I curtsied.

"May your evening be fruitful." He turned on his heel and headed for the punch bowl, where he filled a cup before merging into the crowd of assorted faculty.

I walked in the opposite direction, unsure how I'd manage to find Alex. Temperance's gambit, bringing Dylan as her date, meant he might not have bothered coming. All the same, I had a mission, one best accomplished in shadows I'd never felt comfortable navigating.

On any other night I would have conjured light, but I couldn't draw attention to myself now, especially while Grace still distracted Temperance by shooting dirty looks at her over Crow's shoulder on the dance floor. The music changed to *Three Libras* by A Perfect Circle, a sufficiently seething soundtrack to their rivalry.

"Watch it."

Just like that, I found Alex—by tripping over his feet.

I tumbled to the floor on my back, twisting an ankle on the way and ending up beside him. He didn't catch me, not that I expected it. Ember peeped overhead, swooping toward me. Moments later, she wove to her left instead, as though she'd spotted something. Her white-hot flash of anger made a searing mark in my mind.

"Aren't you getting up, Morgenstern?"

I tried to get up and winced. "Not on my own, so you're stuck with me for now." I grabbed Grace's handbag, pulling it open. Luckily, my eyes had adjusted to the darkness by then.

"Am not." He bent his knees, getting his feet under him. "You know I can't talk to you."

"Wait." I reached in, grabbing the switch. "I've got something for you."

"If it's not a flask of bourbon, I'm not interested."

"It's freedom." I pulled the device out of the bag.

"No," he whimpered.

Alex flung his arms up, crossing them in front of his face, palms out. His eyes widened, whites like ghosts of crescent moons. I realized he thought I'd come here to murder him with a magipsychic device because one like it had hurt him before.

Look what that she-devil is capable of. Who's next?

Three things happened at once. I flipped the switch. Ember dive-bombed him, dropping something long and limp into his lap, and Alex burst into tears, clutching it against his chest and sobbing.

The music covered our confrontation, but it wouldn't for long if this kept up.

"Need help?" Logan stood between us, Doris mewing at whatever Alex held in his arms. No, not a what, a who. His familiar.

He's just a boy under all that venom and self-importance, one who loves his familiar like the rest of you.

"Nurse Smith. For Asceco." I answered. "And we're having a chat later about whatever you couldn't say after the talent show, Alex."

Logan chirped at Doris, who took off running, then held his hand down, and I took it. By the time Nurse Smith arrived, we'd moved far enough away from Alex to avoid getting detained and questioned.

"Why didn't you go to the infirmary with him?" Logan asked.

"We've got to stick around in case Dylan needs us. There's no way he went on this date for real."

Logan glanced around to see who was nearby before saying, "The thingamabob's a one-shot deal."

"We don't need it." I shook my head. "He must have had a plan, like, to get information or something."

Oh, you sweet summer child.

I stopped near the refreshment table. The voice's words confused me. Surely, it didn't think Dylan actually wanted to be around the mean girl? Maybe the best way to ignore it was to do something else.

I decided to give the professor's mysterious extramagus technique another try. Logan stared as I closed my eyes. This time, I managed to visualize a flat, nearly blank horizon like the winter ocean at twilight, and floating across it came the answer to all the turmoil.

Noah and Jonah, dancing together. They gazed into each other's eyes like the rest of the world had ceased to exist.

When I opened my eyes and looked at the dance floor, I saw them in the flesh. Instead of a gaze, their lips met, which caused an unexpected ruckus.

Even at Hawthorn, where we had chaperons and curfews, a kiss like that wouldn't raise faculty hackles. The sound and fury didn't come from the adults in the room.

Temperance Fairbanks let out a frustrated little scream, disgust twisting her face as she dragged Dylan off the dance floor. The humidity level rose as she approached, which meant she was angry enough to conjure without meaning to.

Beside me, Logan narrowed his eyes, humming slightly. The cloying air relaxed its grip as the extra moisture dissipated. Precious the grundylow shot him a dirty look from under Tempe's hair as she retreated to the corner Alex had occupied earlier.

"Uh-oh." Logan winced. "She's gonna get even angrier."

"It's her own fault." Dorian held three cups of punch. "You two look like you need refreshments."

I took one. "Thanks."

"No." Logan refused. "I need to dance." He took both cups from

Dorian and set them on the table, then grabbed his hand. "Come on. I promised you at least one."

I settled into a chair. Logan Pierce was a stress-dancer, so he might stay on the floor with Dorian until the music stopped for the night. I watched everybody on the floor. Even though the as-friends group had been my idea, it seemed like they'd all partnered up out there. Even Cadence had gone to cut a rug with Azrael Ambersmith.

"Hey." The chair beside me creaked.

"Hi, Bar."

"You don't sound happy."

"It's not you."

"I get it. Your dude had a date, even though he accepted the invitation. And she's nothing nice."

"What do you think happened with Crow?"

"He says Grace spent a week begging him to go with her. I don't know why."

You do. But you can hardly tell him about all that.

"So why aren't you out there dancing with Cadence?"

"She said no. Doesn't like me that way."

"Are you okay?"

"I'll live. At least I asked, right?"

"Yeah. You did."

"Who was the guy the nurse took out of here?"

"Alex Onassis."

"Did you know him?"

"He's my ex."

"Are you okay?"

I thought about that for a moment. The mission had been accomplished. We'd thwarted Temperance, but I'd lost my shot at telling Dylan how I felt. She must have decided to use him against us while she could. Maybe the voice had a point about the guitar. The Fairbanks family was extremely wealthy, and they frequented the Lyceum. Bribery with a musical instrument wasn't out of character for them.

But this wasn't over. Tempe could do much worse to Dylan than bribery, and still might. We'd freed Alex in the hope he'd have more information about her larger plans, so I still had work to do. That meant another chance, maybe.

"I'm not, but I'll get better eventually."

"I'm not a good talker. Or a good dancer either." Bar stood. "But I'm around if you need a listener. Tomorrow. I'm heading back to my room."

"Thanks, Bar."

He left.

The music changed to *Everybody Hurts* by REM. I recognized the music from Bubbe's office and it was a huge downer, so a lot of people left the dance floor. I sat, intending to drink the remaining two cups of punch Logan had left on the table.

Grace had other ideas. She sat in the seat Bar had just vacated.

"I'm sorry for pushing the device thing on you at the last minute."

"I managed. But are you going to apologize for the other thing?"

"What do you mean by that?"

"How long did you know about Temperance asking Dylan?"

"About a week. What's the big deal?"

"We're going to have to do all this work again and in as little time. Break's coming up. What if she whammies him?"

"Oh, no, Aliyah." She shook her head. "She won't have to."

"What?" I blinked. "I figured he's here because of that guitar. The only way he could afford that was if she paid for it."

"You're probably right about that." She nodded. "But whatever's been eating him, it's about to go toxic."

"Because he's an extramagus?"

"No." She sighed. "Just, since he got in trouble with the headmaster, he's been on a downward spiral."

"You noticed, and you still refused to apologize?"

"I can't lose face. None of us can afford that."

"It must be so hard being popular."

"Actually, it is. I have to look flawless, can't mess anything up, and have to say the perfect thing in the exact tone. I thought you'd under-stand because you have it harder as an extramagus."

"Boo-fricking-hoo, Grace. You chose to do the It Girl thing. I never opted in."

"I didn't know it'd be like this. Fake image, fake boyfriends, fake everything. At least you get to be real."

"You know what being real is? It's helping your friends. Making sure they don't fall so far they hurt themselves. How many times did you thank me for being there last year?"

"You know. You saved my life."

"And you didn't save Dylan's? Why? Because you used to be a couple?"

"He's not suicidal."

"What do you think Tempe's about then? Handing out guitars with no strings?"

"Hate crimes." She hung her head. "Against half the people on this campus. Shit. I've been wrong this whole time."

"It's okay. We can fix it."

"What do we do?"

"Finish this dance." I stood, and she joined me. "At least you do. I'm going back to our room and making a list."

"I'm not sure I want to be here either. Crow's intense."

"Then dance with someone else. Cadence would probably love to take him off your hands."

"Yeah, I owe her an apology, along with some other people."

"Do you want me to go with you?"

"Nah, I've got this. You go make the list."

We parted ways. As I headed toward the stairs, I ran into Faith and Hal.

"It worked." I held the bag out toward him.

"Great." He took it. "I'll be tweaking it again over the break. We might want it again in the spring."

"Are you leaving already?" Faith asked. "You barely danced."

"I did plenty. I'm exhausted." I yawned.

"So are we," Hal said.

We headed up the stairs together.

CHAPTER EIGHT

The next morning, Logan knocked on our door. Grace had come in sometime after I'd gone to sleep, and he wanted to see her. Apparently, he'd danced a hole into his shoe, but she wasn't remotely ready to wake up. We left his dress shoes in my room and went down to the café for pastry and magical bean juice. The place was deserted except for us.

"So, how'd it go with Dorian?" I asked, settling into one of the tufted chairs by the fireplace. It wasn't lit, but I fixed that as we sat down.

"It didn't." Logan stared into his Americano.

"Oh?" I dunked a biscotti in my latte.

"I think I liked the idea of Dorian more than, you know, *him*." He glanced at his chocolate croissant. "If that makes sense."

"No, I get it. So you were stress-dancing?"

"Nobody's ever called it that." He snorted. "But yeah. I wore him out."

"Who'd you dance with after that?"

"Grace, and then a guy from Gallow's Hill. He had no trouble keeping up, even though he had two left feet. Big guy, but nice. I think we're going to be friends." Logan finally took a bite of his croissant.

"Bar?"

"How'd you know?"

"Lucky guess." I dunked my cookie again. "What happened with Cadence?"

"Oh, she's back together with Crow."

"Well then, the evening turned out all right for her, at least."

"And Alex."

"But he was in tears last time we saw him."

"We helped him, though. He must be better off now, so let's visit him."

I had my doubts, but the only way to know for sure was directly from him. We finished our pastries and caffeinated drinks, got a blueberry muffin and herbal tea to go, then headed down the ramp to the infirmary. It was quiet, and Nurse Smith wasn't at his desk. Ezekiel Brown, the vampire CNA, was on duty instead.

"Hi, Zeke."

"Mr. Pierce. Miss Morgenstern. What do you need?"

"We're checking on Alex Onassis," Logan said.

"Ah, I remember." He nodded. "It was your familiar who alerted the nurse to his condition. He's here. I'll see if he's awake."

Moments later, Zeke returned, nodding. He opened the door to one of the exam rooms, and we went inside. Alex sat up on the edge of a bed, his familiar curled up in his lap, asleep. Despite the night in the infirmary, he didn't look well-rested, and he sneered at us.

Logan smiled anyway, setting the tea and muffin on the bedside table. I stood there with my arms crossed, leaning in the doorway. In this case, Logan was the optimist. We'd done the right thing for Alex, even if we'd had our own motives. I wasn't waiting for an about-face.

"Why are you being so nice to me?" He snorted, but quietly.

"Not nice, good," I answered. "There's a difference. One's for people you like, the other's doing the right thing for whoever needs it."

"That's fair."

"Exactly." Logan nodded. Doris paced over to the bed, hopped up, and sat there peering at Asceco as he slept.

"I'll rephrase. Why did you help me?"

"You needed it. Wasn't that why you went to Aliyah twice?" Logan answered.

"There's got to be a *káti gia káti*." He sighed, shaking his head. "Quid pro quo."

"If it makes you feel better, fine." I tilted my head. "What were you trying to tell me up in the light booth?"

"Oh." He paled, making the circles under his eyes look darker than before. "Not here."

"I'm not going into your room or letting you in mine."

"I meant off-campus."

"Fine. When?"

"How about we walk you to the train?" Logan offered. "When you leave for break, I mean."

"That works." He nodded. "But there's something I can say that you need to know. About *her*."

"Go on." I waved my hand, trying to look nonchalant even though his impending warning spooked me. Ember stirred on my shoulder, peeping softly.

"Don't let her bring Dylan back to New York with her." He sighed, closing his eyes. "I went at Thanksgiving. It was all downhill from there."

Logan and I stood silent and staring. His jaw dropped. Had his gut crashed too, like mine? The danger was clear to both of us, at least.

"But how?" I finally managed. "He's barely talking to most of us."

"I have some ideas," Logan said. "Whatever we try, we'll do our best."

"Thanks for the snack, Pierce. Now leave me alone. I'm going back to sleep."

We parted ways upstairs, with Logan heading back to his room. It had something to do with those ideas, which he didn't explain to me. I spent the rest of the day in the gym, running the track and doing drills. It was the only thing that came close to quelling my new and unwelcome sense of foreboding.

Everyone spent the last week before break studying. Lab didn't have exams, but we'd be tested on lecture material. The second-year students worked overtime on catching up. We'd been awfully distracted. Dylan refused help from everyone except Logan, who became his constant companion. Dorian gave them space, tagging along with me instead.

It eased my fears about winter break. I'd come to trust Logan Pierce like family. He'd do his best to convince Dylan to stay on campus for the winter. Alex's untold story hung over our heads like razor wire, and my fraying self-control made my hands glow at random. The last thing I needed was to stir up any extramagus hatred.

I wore myself out physically, both at the gym and in the baths, swimming morning and night. If I was too tired for anxiety, maybe it'd leave me alone. Faith noticed. She must have squealed on me to Izzy because she showed up on Wednesday night, towel in hand.

"Have you tried meditation?" She gave me a hand out of the pool.

"No. The last thing I want is more time to think."

"It's not like that." Izzy tossed the towel at my head. "I do it all the time. At least try it. I don't like how thin you're getting."

"Excuse me?" I blinked.

"You've lost what looks like ten pounds in a week. I can see your ribs."

I stood at the mirror. Hip bones jutted under the hem on my tank-ini, which draped a little in front. I agreed to try meditating but during break. I stopped swimming in the mornings and added protein smoothies at breakfast and lunch to appease her.

The exam on Monday was the least of my worries. I answered every question with little trouble. Much of it was on topics we'd studied on our own time.

People leaving campus packed and prepared. Most were heading out on Tuesday, with extramural students taking a detour by their campuses before traveling out of town. Alex's flight back to Greece was a Monday night red-eye, so he left campus after lunch. I waited ten minutes, then helped Logan gather bags for Bubbe's, which was our pretense for leaving when we did. We'd meet Alex at the Witch's Brew.

"How did it go with Dylan?"

"He's staying here." Logan pulled the door to the hallway open. "But I didn't convince him. Noah did."

I blinked. We continued down the hall, pushing through the exit into the street. We paused to put on gloves and hats, and Logan continued as we walked down Essex Street.

"Your brother asked Dylan to play some gigs with him in town over the break. Paying ones." Logan paused, adjusting the strap on his satchel. "Apparently, Tempe bought that Paul Reed Smith guitar Dylan's had since the talent show. Noah made it clear he didn't like that."

I nodded. "I guess Dylan respects him, then."

Alex stood outside the coffee shop. He'd been inside though, because he had hot chocolates for both of us. When I asked why he bothered, he said, "It's only money."

We went the rest of the way down Essex Street, turning right on Washington toward the train station. The streets were largely deserted, the only people hurrying through the cold on brisk errands. He made sure nobody was nearby before speaking.

"She wants to make an example of a lesser extrahuman."

"'Lesser?'" I stared at him.

"Look, I don't know how else to say what that means." He sighed. "I'm not sure who or how, but whatever she does to them, it'll be extremely humiliating. Probably painful, too."

"Any idea who she might choose? Or when she'll do it?"

"The Craft Expo, maybe?" Logan asked.

"Spirit Week and Bishop's Row are both higher-profile events. Probably during one of those." He shuddered. "She knows how to bide her time."

"Was she always planning this?"

"If so, she didn't tell me until after Thanksgiving." He reached inside his coat, stroking Asceco's head. She hissed softly in response. "When she had leverage."

"Did she poison Clementine? And Seth?"

"Yeah. Somehow, she used poison that felt just like her roommate's. I don't know how she did it because she insists she's not an extramagus."

I nodded. "I've got that figured out."

"Can you sense each other or something?" Alex blinked. "On second thought, don't answer that."

"Did you know she had a secret boyfriend?"

"Oh, gods, yes. Asceco smelled him on her all the time. I didn't care." His breath caught in his throat. "I was never into her, but I was okay with us using each other. Tolerated all her lying. But then she—"

"We know she hurt you." Logan patted his arm. "Faith told us how bad she could be."

"She's half my size, but her magic's like a tsunami. And that grundylow." He shivered. "We were lopsided from the start, but once she had the upper hand, it got brutal."

"What did he smell like?" Logan asked. "The boyfriend, I mean?"

"I don't see how that'll help. Dragonets and mercats don't have the same senses as a basilisk."

"Noah's got a tallin," I offered.

"Oh, gods, he's not in on this?" Alex's attempted laugh turned into a sob. "Not after what I did to him last year?"

"My brother holds crazy grudges, so no." I sighed. "We're trying to find out who he is."

"I can talk to Asceco," Logan said. "I've got a weird ability. If that's okay with you."

"Rare. And yeah, okay." Alex nodded, opening his coat again. Logan and Asceco peered at each other for almost a minute, sticking their tongues out a few times in the process.

"All set." He nodded. "Thanks, Alex."

"No." He shook his head. "Don't thank me for throwing a thimble of water on a house fire I helped set."

"I don't take returns on thank yous." Logan grinned. "It's a big gesture, coming from you."

"We're even now, so don't expect any more."

"Noted." I jerked my chin at the train, which had just pulled in. "That's your ride. Don't miss it."

He nodded, then turned his back on us and headed up the stairs to the platform.

"Have a good break," Logan called after him.

He threw one hand up in farewell and got on the train. After that, Logan and I headed to Bubbe's, where we stowed his bags in the spare room. She was busy with a patient, so we only said hello and goodbye before heading back to campus and having dinner with our friends.

The next day was a flurry of goodbyes. Arick and Lena went to the airport at the same time since they were on the same Lufthansa flight to Frankfurt, where they'd catch trains to Bergen and Genoa. Hailey and Bailey caught their Acela to New York, the same one Temperance took, though they got on a different car. Kitty and Eston left together, headed to Portland so he could meet her mothers. They all departed after breakfast.

Faith stayed on campus that year, along with Hal, Dylan, Lee, and Grace, who promised to keep her from getting bored. Dorian got on the commuter rail after lunch. Providence wasn't far and he missed his parents, but he promised to let us know when he was on the way back so we could meet him at Salem station.

Elanor stayed longest, leaving while the rest of us were on the way to dinner. She was almost at the door, where Noah waited to walk her out. I thought she'd leave without saying goodbye, but she turned and sprinted toward Logan, lifting him off the floor in a bear hug. Their eyes were bright and shiny, though they didn't weep.

"You take care of my baby brother, Morgenstern," she told me.

I nodded and she was gone.

Noah came to me in the living room after breakfast on the third day of break. Logan and I were playing video games.

"I'm in love," he said. "With Jonah Arnold."

"That's awesome." I hugged him. "I'm so happy for you!"

"We're going on a date tonight, to the movies."

"Cool!" Logan smiled. "We're walking around to look at everyone's holiday decorations."

"So, you two?" Noah raised an eyebrow. "Like, alone together?"

"No." Logan shook his head. "Most of the gang from school, plus Izzy and Cadence."

"No Crow?" He didn't ask about Dylan, who hadn't been over yet.

"They broke up again." I shrugged. "I kinda hope they stay that way," I said, and I told Noah about what I'd heard at the Lyceum.

"That's the Merlini family business for you. Cadence can do better."

But she didn't. They got back together that night.

Most of break went on the same way, hanging around with friends and doing whatever the weather and our budgets allowed around Salem. I kept offering Logan some of my allowance, but he refused.

"I'm working for Bubbe. She's paying me. It's only a little, but enough for pocket money."

Noah and I invited everyone still at Hawthorn over for the first night of Hanukkah, the Festival of Lights. And Jonah, who couldn't share our meal with us or come until an hour after sunset. Mom, Dad, and Bubbe agreed to have dinner first, despite our usual tradition.

Hal and Faith were in Boston at the hospital, but everybody else showed up. Even Dylan, who seemed happy to be there all through dinner. That made sense, considering how much he loved food.

"These are amazing!" he exclaimed over dessert. "What are they?"

"*Sufganya.*" I passed him another fried confection of jelly-filled dough. "Noah made them."

"Even better."

Since the holiday was all about hope and endurance, I wanted him to have a good time. So I went to a lot of effort, making another batch of *sufganya*. He said he wasn't hungry anymore, but put most of it in his backpack for later.

After that, I made sure to include him in the group playing dreidel. The rules were simple enough for everyone to follow, though Grace confused the letters on most of her spins.

"That was *Nun*." I tapped the Hebrew letter. "You get nothing."

"Sorry, thought it was *Gimmel*." She put back the pile of foil-wrapped chocolate gelt she'd raked in by mistake.

"Easy mistake to make." I shrugged. "They're similar. Noah used to deliberately mix them up."

"Hey!" he protested. "I was six."

"Yeah. You're all grown up now." Dylan grinned, watching his spin. "*Hei*, right? That means I take half?"

"Uh-huh." I nodded.

"Do they all mean something?" Lee picked the top up, turning it in his hand to look at the letters before taking his turn.

"*Nes gadol hayah sham*." Noah chanted.

"A great miracle happened here." I translated. "After Judah won the temple back, the oil lasted eight nights instead of one. It's why we make all the fried food."

"Why didn't they just make more oil?" Lee spun, watched, then shrugged. "*Nun*." He passed the dreidel to me.

"They couldn't let the light go out, or the temple would have stayed desecrated." I spun. "*Shin*. Put one in."

I tossed a piece of gelt into the pot between us and passed the dreidel, but before Logan could spin, someone knocked on the door. Noah jumped up, opening it to let Jonah in. They hugged, pecking each other on both cheeks like they do in Europe, but they held hands as Noah led him out of the living room and into the kitchen to meet our parents.

After that, Dylan's mood soured. He collected his things and made excuses, preparing to leave. I tried to stop him.

"At least stay for the *Menorah*."

"Yeah, Dylan," Grace added. "Remember what we talked about?"

He blinked. "All right, fine. But as soon as that's done, I'm going."

We gathered in the dining room by the window facing the back yard. Dad set the candles out beside the matchbook, one for the first night and the other the *shamash*, which was the candle in the middle that brought light to the others. On the first night, we said three blessings.

"*Baruch Atah Adonai Elohenu Melech haolam asher kideshanu bemitzvotav vetzivanu lehadlik ner Chanukah*," Dad sang.

"Blessed are You, Lord our God, King of the universe, who has sanctified us with His commandments and commanded us to kindle the Chanukah light," Noah murmured beside Jonah, squeezing his hand.

"*Baruch Atah Adonai Elohenu Melech Haolam sheasa nisim laavotenu bayamim hahem bizman hazeh*," Bubbe sang. Logan joined in, pronouncing the Hebrew almost exactly like my grandma. He must have asked for her help practicing.

"Wow," I said. He blushed.

"Blessed are You, Lord our God, King of the universe, who performed miracles for our forefathers in those days at this time." Dylan recited under his breath, arms crossed over his chest. "I studied too."

"Shh." Lee elbowed him.

"It's okay. I remember what it was like, learning these when I was your age. Right here in this room, too," Mom said. Then she sang the third blessing. "*Baruch Atah Adonai Elohenu Melech Haolam shehecheyanu vekiyimanu vehigianu lizman hazeh*."

"Blessed are You, Lord our God, King of the universe, who has granted us life, sustained us, and enabled us to reach this occasion." I translated for Grace, who sighed, nodding. I figured the third prayer, said only on the first night, would resonate especially well with her.

My father struck a match, lit the *shamash*, and touched the flame to the wick on the first candle. It sat vigil for a moment until Dad set the *shamash* in the middle. The flames stabilized, pushing the darkness back from the window if only just a little.

The flames guttered, flickering briefly in the wake of Dylan's passage. He left without saying goodbye. Grace and I both glanced over our shoulders, listening to the front door closing behind him.

"I apologized. We're good."

"What's his problem, then?"

"Beats me. Ask your brother. They hang out all the time."

I didn't. Not because I spaced and forgot to, either.

It's because you don't want to. Not really.

Being with my family and friends let me ignore the Evil Inside Voice for a good while longer.

CHAPTER NINE

Classes should have gotten back to normal after the break in January. Everyone was back, including the extramural groups from the other schools. Something felt off, though, like the stillness ahead of a Nor'easter. I resumed my frantic levels of physical training from the week before break. This time I avoided Izzy so she wouldn't notice.

Dylan trained at the same time, conjuring and throwing orbs in the middle of the gym. I circled him, running around my crush in an ironic parallel to avoiding my emotions. I'd ruined last year's team dynamic with relationship drama. Fear of the same outcome stopped me.

Maybe it wasn't for the best. I hadn't felt this unstable since I'd first started hearing the Evil Inside Voice and randomly conjuring solar magic. I needed something to control, and training, especially with Bishop's Row coming at the end of February, was the most constructive option.

I'd have to stick to a strategy of steady meals. That shouldn't have been hard at a boarding school with scheduled dining, or so I thought.

The unease I'd witnessed in Professor Luciano had grown so much that even Dorian noticed. Usually sharp and quick like Ember on a sunny day, our teacher reminded me of flat soda. By Monday of the third week, I couldn't stand it and headed to my room after Lab. I sat cross-legged on the floor, clearing my mind to see what showed up. Instead of visualizing him or any classmate, I got the Evil Inside Voice.

It's the poisonings. You forgot to meet with the headmaster.

"Crap on a crap cracker."

I stood up so quickly I got dizzy. Leaning on my desk, I waited for the feeling to pass. The moment it did, I rushed out of the room, Ember flapping along behind me until she managed to grab my blazer and cling on. In moments, my feet carried me down the stairs, which I'd activated for an even bigger speed boost. The lobby flew by in a blur.

A convenient column helped me turn the corner ahead of the academic wing, which led to the headmaster's office. I skidded to a stop, reaching out to pull the door open. As my fingers made contact with it, I heard a voice from the shadows to my right.

"That was fast." Hal stepped forward. "I just sent Nin to your room to fetch you."

"She's there alone, then." I panted to catch my breath. "Because I'm here for my own reasons."

"Hmm." He tilted his head. "That might get complicated. My dad wants to ask you a few questions."

"As long as it's not about Professor Luciano."

"It is, actually. He's already in there." He sighed. "I've got to fetch Nin. Good luck in there, Aliyah."

My hand trembled as it reached to open the door, almost like it wasn't part of me anymore. The wood was feverishly warm, or maybe my hand was cold, but I pulled it open anyway.

Once inside, I sat in the chair to the right of my professor. The other one was already occupied by Professor DeBeer.

"Miss Morgenstern, perhaps you can enlighten us."

"I'll try, Headmaster."

"Professor DeBeer thinks she saw Professor Luciano in the café after your last period on the day Clementine was poisoned. Hal tells me that you were the last student to leave the laboratory that day. Do you happen to remember which way he went after closing up the room?"

"I don't." I sighed. "I didn't see him lock up."

"Then we're at an impasse, I'm afraid. Unless you know anything that could help us clear this up."

"I might. What sort of thing do you mean?"

"The whereabouts of any ice or poison magus, especially if you saw one of each together near the cafe it would be helpful, in addition to any troubling statements they might have made."

My brain went into overdrive. Alex had come down from upstairs. Dorian and Lena had gone straight to the infirmary with me. Dylan was working in the café but they already knew that and had cleared him. Were there any faculty besides Luciano with poison? And what about ice?

"I only saw Dylan." How was I supposed to help Professor Luciano? And why was he under suspicion?

What about that stained glass mural? Fire with poison ice? Am I ringing a bell?

My professor had taught me to sense magic as an extramagus as though he'd done it himself. Great-Uncle Noah hadn't gotten his second element until long after graduation, in the Coast Guard. After Filberto Luciano was back in Italy, writing letters overseas. My eyes widened.

"I certainly didn't see Professor Luciano in there. He wasn't in the lobby, not before or after Familiar Bonding. Professor DeBeer must have been mistaken."

"How dare you?" She whirled, staring daggers at me. "Call in a different student, sir. Miss Morgenstern's got a natural bias."

I knew what she meant but refused to disclose my revelation about the man who in kinder times might have been my great uncle-in-law.

"Which was what you said earlier about my son, Professor DeBeer."

Block her throw.

"The lobby was packed. There should be lots of students to ask."

Not like that. With Seth. But don't rat your friends out.

"Another familiar was poisoned a month later." Headmaster Hawkins raised an eyebrow. "Was Professor Luciano there for that?"

I shook my head. "No."

"Where did it happen, then?"

These waters are shark-infested. Tread them carefully.

"I'm not sure. You'd have to ask Faith. I wasn't with her when it happened."

"Then how do you know he wasn't with her?"

Don't lie, just skirt the truth. It's the only way to protect them all.

"The same way I knew Seth was in trouble. Something I tried after a lot of research."

Both true. Now digress.

"I'm an extramagus. We have this quirk, sort of. To sense, like, disturbances in the Force."

Good job.

"Is that true? Can extramagi trace the flow of magic?"

"Yes, Headmaster." Professor Luciano nodded. "Like tanuki trace luck, though the ability to manipulate it is limited to their particular elements. And of course, their coincidental drawback."

He meant the limitation in power. Every extramagus was supposed to have one. Uncle Richard's was the only one I'd heard about in detail. It was geographic, limiting everything but his initial element of fire to Rhode Island.

"Thank the gods for those." Professor DeBeer traced a sigil I couldn't identify in the air.

"Have you discovered your drawback yet, Miss Morgenstern?"

"No, but I haven't tried."

"Noted." Headmaster Hawkins waved his hand at the door. "Miss Morgenstern, Professor Luciano. You're both free to go. I've got more to discuss with Professor DeBeer, however."

"This isn't over, Lucy." Susan DeBeer glared. "We'll find out who's been inappropriate with students eventually, and you're not off my radar yet."

I opened the door for my teacher and closed it behind him, too. He looked wearier than before but not as weighed down.

"What did she mean, inappropriate with students?" I led him to the other end of the short hallway, away from the door. "If it's about the dance, I'll go in there and explain it to her."

"There was an anonymous tip." He leaned against the column I'd used to pivot with earlier.

"And of course, she blames the ex—" I cleared my throat. "Er, ex-boyfriend of my great-uncle first."

"Ah." He nodded. "You understand."

"Yeah, but why didn't you just tell me?" I scratched my head, a spot behind my left ear. It stung like a slice of jalapeno except not on the tongue.

"Didn't I?" He raised an eyebrow.

"I'm not talking about Noah the elder." The stinging sensation intensified like angry bees.

"Neither am I, but I can't directly mention the other thing."

"Why?" I reached up again. The stinging buzz ramped up, along with a strange whine in my ear.

"Sealed records."

The bottom dropped out of my world, and I toppled. The professor wasn't quick enough to catch me. The last thing I remembered for a while was concern creasing his face and Ember's frantic shriek.

I woke in the infirmary with Ember's upside-down head before me as she peered into my face.

"Peep?"

"Yeah, I'm awake." I sighed, turning my head to look around. Hal was in the next bed for his infusion, Faith by his side.

"What are you in for?" Hal asked. "Never mind. We were here when they brought you, so we know."

"I don't."

"You collapsed." Faith picked a paper cup with a lid and a straw off my bedside table and handed it to me. "Dehydration, stress, and insufficient caloric intake. Don't get up, you're on an IV."

"What about Professor Luciano? Is he okay?" I peered at the cup, unable to determine its contents.

"Besides worrying about you, he's fine." Hal pointed at the beverage. "It's banana berry. Jonah brought it; he says it's full of potassium."

"Jonah?" I took a sip. It felt like heaven and tasted like manna from that neighborhood too. I drank more. "Noah's boyfriend? Jonah Arnold?"

"Yeah." Faith answered. "Noah was with him, rolling his eyes and everything. Jonah insisted it was Noah's idea."

"No way." I blinked.

"Yeah." Hal grinned. "He actually got Noah to admit he cares."

"Wow. Sounds familiar."

Hal smiled like a window full of sunbeams while Faith blushed.

"We've got the Craft Expo, then Spirit Week with all the school monarch business and games in less than a month." Faith tapped the cup, then pointed at me. "Drink up, and keep a food journal or something. Don't make me come off reserves and steal your glory."

"Okay."

"I'd love to tell you not to be a stranger, Aliyah." Hal grinned. "But I don't want you visiting during infusion time like this again. Just walk in like everyone else."

We all had a laugh at that. I was good to go at about the same time they were, so we left together. The cafeteria was closed, so I got another smoothie and some croissants at the cafe and ate them in my room. Grace was out, where I didn't know. Popularity kept her busy.

I didn't wait up for my roommate. After brushing my teeth and getting into PJs, I remembered what the professor had said right before I passed out.

Sealed records. Dorian had mentioned those in his story. The unidentified male conspirator had mentioned them also, which lined up with Tempe's secret boyfriend. Was this a clue that could reveal his identity?

I got into bed. Just before dropping off to sleep, I thought I had it, but when my eyes closed, all I dreamed of was Bishop's Row, accompanied by the sound of regulation whistles.

The rest of January flew by. I had to share my extra time in the gym with each school's cheer squad. I hadn't thought of them since the beginning of the year, which seemed like it had been before the Common Era, but they persisted, cranking music and practicing routines to commands shouted by their coaches.

The Hawthorn group was Coach Chen's project. He'd handed the reins of captain over to Logan Pierce, who had way more dancing talent than I'd imagined. The twins, Kitty, Grace, and Arick filled out the rest of the team. The second day they practiced during my track time, Alex showed up. Coach Chen and Logan spent a good twenty minutes in conversation I couldn't hear, and he ended up on the squad.

Messing's faculty coach was a willowy brunette woman with a pixie by her side, which meant she was a psychic summoner and that she knew performance art since pixies loved song and dance. The student captain was Jacinta, a memory psychic cousin of Azrael's. I didn't know why she passed wristbands to each squad member, but when they performed their routine for the first time at levels approaching perfect, I understood. She'd impressed the routine into the bands, likely with her coach's help.

Gallows Hill blew me away. I stopped running a few times just to watch them. Cadence was the captain, and instead of dancing, she'd leaned heavily into gymnastics. Her squad of shifters and changelings practiced backflips and danced on their hands, tossing each other into the air on multiple occasions. Stephanie Hawkins was technically coaching, but she left everything to Cadence, who clearly knew her squad's abilities.

Logan burned the candle at both ends. He had to captain the cheer squad but also finish his paintings for the Craft Expo, which came first. I checked on him, eventually settling into a routine of getting smoothies between meals.

"Something's got to give." Logan sighed. "I can't do everything."

"Grace said something like that before break." I twirled the straw in my banana berry smoothie. "Why not delegate? Nobody can do your artwork for you, but how about appointing a lieutenant for the cheer squad?"

"That's not a bad idea." He perked up. "They all know the routine now. If someone could supervise them running through it, I could spend some extra time in the Creatives room. But who?"

"How about Kitty? She's got experience keeping people on track, what with Truncheons and Flagons every week."

"I'll ask her. Thanks!"

After that, I saw less of Logan in the gym at odd hours, and he seemed more content. He finished all three of his paintings in time for the Expo. It was held in the gym, so I let Ember fly around all she wanted.

We'd all been encouraged to dress business casual or better. Logan chose his navy-blue suit, the one Grace had made, and he told everyone who his designer was, including the student visitors and the judges who came by to view his work. I heard it all, sitting with my brick design kiln-fired mugs at the next table.

"You're being too nice," Alex interrupted. "Stop it."

"It's true, though." Logan shrugged.

"Don't promote yourself, then." Alex sauntered off. "Doesn't matter to me."

"Maybe he's right." I sighed. "I don't like admitting that, but this expo is about showing your own work."

"I'm not going to stop saying nice things that are true about my friends just because there are judges, Aliyah."

"I get it."

After that, I let Logan be himself, but I took a page out of his book and talked his paintings up to anyone who even glanced at my pottery. Maybe I was biased because one depicted Ember stuck in my hair. Even though Logan hadn't been there when it happened, he'd loved the story enough to spend weeks painting his vision of it.

Everybody expected the press to be there. We'd been given release forms, with one specific publication listed: the Extrahuman Examiner, the social paper Cadence's mother worked for. She clicked around the room on heels so high and spindly they reminded me of church spires, taking notes and pictures with a MagPad, the only device guaranteed to work in the Under and its adjacent places.

She stopped in front of Logan's table, too far away for him to make conversation. I watched her tapping furiously on the screen, pausing between sentences like she was conversing with someone else. In the end, she didn't talk to Logan. Or me, either.

"That's weird." I scratched my head.

"Doris said the same thing." Logan reached down to pat her.

"Peep!" Ember darted through the air, making a figure eight above my head before landing on my table, where she hopped up and down, peeping excitedly at Logan.

"Oh!" He blinked. "Really, Ember?"

Before I could ask what just happened, a man approached the table. He wore his tan tweed suit like an afterthought, but the smile on his face as he gazed at Logan's work was genuine.

"Hello!" He stuck out his hand. "I'm Jim Howard from the Boston Globe. Mrs. DelMar sent me."

"Logan Pierce." They shook. "Are you a judge?"

"I edit the extrahuman Interest section. Every year, we do a series on student art in Massachusetts, and I'd like to interview you about those paintings if you don't mind."

"Of course! I mean, I don't mind at all."

"I'll keep an eye on your table, Logan." I grinned.

Logan led Mr. Howard toward the café, where they ordered coffee and sat down. He ended up missing the judges. By the time he returned, they'd tallied the scores, and Headmaster Hawkins was ready to make the announcement.

Even though no other artist had gotten press attention, Logan placed third. He stayed up at the podium to wait for the other winners and cheered each of them. Grace came in second with her fashion collection, which didn't surprise me. Neither did the first place winner, Azrael Ambersmith.

I had a look after the fact at his chess set, crafted from myriad found items and upcycled materials. It followed the traditional faerie division of Seelie and Unseelie, facing each other across the board. Most chess sets along a fae theme didn't include any other extrahumans, but Azrael's was diverse. Surprising to many, but not me, who'd known him for so long.

His pawns were shifters; wolves on the Unseelie side faced lions across the board. The rooks were magi, representing fire on the Seelie side across from ice. Knights were familiars, golden dragonets countering Unseelie jet gryphons. Clairvoyant bishops carried satchels and brandished cards at Unseelie telekinetics with projectiles hovering over their heads.

The monarchs took my breath away. The Seelie king had golden hair, with eyes glancing to one side. His queen's hair was longer and ruddy, and she faced the board with grim determination. I had no idea who'd inspired Azrael, but they were clearly patterned after people he knew.

I recognized the Unseelie king immediately, though I wasn't sure how Azrael had managed to capture both love and pain on such a small face. I put a hand over my chest, blinking back tears.

"It's Hal."

"And of course his queen is Faith," Grace murmured as she pointed at the figure, which wore the dress she'd made for our friend.

"Why?"

"Az wanted to give them a tribute after he heard nobody was doing stained glass this year."

"How?" I sniffled. "He doesn't go around talking about it."

"That's my fault," Grace said. "I couldn't help it, Aliyah. I told Azrael about Hal's illness back in October."

"No, I understand." I hugged her. "You really care about him, huh?"

"We've got to keep fighting." She sniffled, arms still around me. "It doesn't matter how I feel."

"It does. The whole reason we're working so hard is so everyone can be who they are and follow their hearts, including you."

"You're too nice." She pulled back, looking me in the eye.

Déjà vu.

"Promise me you'll be kind to yourself. And soon, Grace."

"When I'm sure we're winning, yeah."

We dropped our arms, letting go. After that, I worked even harder.

CHAPTER TEN

Noah came out to run during the last week of January. It reminded me of how we used to circle Salem Commons through middle school, with one exception: he smiled almost constantly. I was sure Jonah's presence on the bleachers had something to do with it.

My brother's vampire boyfriend was on Messing's team, but that didn't stop him from cheering us on and supplying us with water when we needed it. He sat with Hal, who'd taken to timing us.

"Why aren't you training?" I asked him between laps.

"I don't need to do cardio anymore." He grinned.

"So why help the competition?" I raised an eyebrow.

"I don't see it that way. Extramurals are about coming together and recognizing how we're all awesome."

"I feel the same," Hal added. "We're stronger together."

"Thanks for the smoothie, by the way."

"Glad to help. Before this happened, I trained too hard a few times myself."

"I'm glad you and Noah found each other, Jonah."

"I'm a lucky guy. My boyfriend's amazing, and his sister approves."

"You've got one up on Hal." Faith strode over. "And I hear you on the amazing boyfriend thing. I might have to fight you if you say Noah's the best, though."

"We can agree to disagree," Jonah replied. "Until one of them ends up as Hawthorn's Spirit Week Monarch."

We all had a laugh.

Then Faith joined our supplemental track runs.

I tried to ignore the Monarch business, which wasn't easy with Grace as my roommate. She was campaigning for one of the two Hawthorn crowns, of course.

"We can't let Tempe win this."

"After all the times we thwarted her socially, do you even think she has a chance?"

"I wouldn't put it past her to get votes by coercion."

I thought about Professor Luciano's sealed record and had to agree. She had access to reputation-damaging information through her conspirator. Dorian was supposed to be investigating the secret boyfriend, and I approached him that day at lunch and cut right to the chase.

"Have you found anything in Coach Pickman's files? About you-know-who's boyfriend?"

"Nobody seems likely, last time I checked."

"When was that, Dorian."

"December." He winced. "Sorry. I'm not sure whether you feel this, but something's been off since we came back."

"I have. It's distracting, but we can't drop the ball. If we do, the abusive bigot will terrorize everyone."

"Yeah, I know, but we've defeated her pretty soundly on all fronts. I'm not sure what more we can do."

"Grace's latest thing is making sure she doesn't get a Monarch crown."

"That's easy."

"How? When Grace is the only major candidate, the second crown could go to anyone."

"You make Alex Onassis a poster child."

"Huh?"

"She pretty much brutalized the poor kid, and her entire year knows it. They're scared of her, so we need to either make them brave or humiliate her. Which do you want?"

"Bravery." I shook my head. "She's the horrible one, so we go high."

"We remind them that Alex Onassis survived her bullshit."

"He'll never admit weakness, not even to say he came through it alive."

"Someone else should speak for him—a charismatic individual who stands up when it matters."

"You?"

"Nah, I'm a coward. I'm talking about you."

"Bishop's Row practice is no joke. You've got spare time."

"I gave you the idea. Find someone else."

I tried but came up with nothing. Eston and Logan weren't built for that kind of social maneuvering. Kitty was way too nice to pull off public criticism. Lee was Switzerland. In Tempe's own year, the only people I trusted were Lena, who was too timid, and Arick, who needed to study. I asked Izzy for advice.

"Yeah, no." She stared at the cards spread across the floor in her room. "It's not going to work without Dorian."

"Or me?"

"No. You can't pull it off. See this Empress reversed? It might even backfire and make Tempe look sympathetic. You're Alex's ex, and you're intimidating, Aliyah."

"So, how do I convince Dorian to buck up?"

She flipped The Fool reversed and stared at it. "You don't. It's up to him. The only thing you can reasonably do is say you didn't find anyone and leave it at that."

I followed her advice, expecting the worst, which I assumed happened when Dorian shook his head at my news. Right afterward, I saw him talking to Alex in the hall.

Neither of them came forward with a public statement, but something happened—a rumor about Temperance, one that had everyone laughing at her. He'd gone with humiliation after all.

Arick told me the story. Tempe had threatened Alex while they dated, forcing him to dress and act like a gnome during their intimate time. I knew that wasn't true, but it was an extremely damaging rumor to an open magisupremacist.

Snickers and snorts followed Tempe everywhere. Her face seemed constantly red and her fists were eternally clenched. Dorian had utterly wrecked her reputation, along with any chance at a Monarch crown.

He's kicked a hornet's nest. Beware her sting.

I tried to corner Dorian, hoping he'd get another reading from Izzy, but he avoided me. I wasn't sure why. I couldn't even talk to him long enough for a simple warning.

The votes were in and the results given on the last Friday in February. At the end of Spirit Week, they'd crown the Monarchs at the Cheer Squad competition, the night before the Bishop's Row games. The extramural guests and the entire Hawthorn student body sat in the gym's bleachers, waiting. Stephanie Hawkins made the announcement for Gallows Hill.

"We've heard your voices, and they chose two of our most talented. Your Monarchs are Cadence DelMar and Brianna Collins!"

The girls hurried off the bleachers, rushing to her side to curtsy and bow. Once the cheers died down, they moved back to their seats to let Dean Adelphi make the announcement for Messing Academy.

"You're all Monarchs in my book, but the students representing you are Jonah Arnold and Isabella Mendez!" All the Messing Academy kids snapped their fingers instead of clapping like they were at a poetry slam instead of a pep rally. In moments, cheers from both Gallows Hill and Hawthorn drowned them out. That made sense because Jonah and Izzy both moved in circles outside their schools.

You could have heard a pin drop as Headmaster Hawkins stepped to the middle of the gym. He held the paper with the results almost like an afterthought, and I was shocked by his announcement.

"At Hawthorn Academy, we see ourselves as an extended family. That's why I'm so pleased to announce that our crowns go to a pair of blood relatives."

I blinked because Grace Dubois was an only child.

"Noah and Aliyah Morgenstern!"

It was all I could do to keep from tripping over my own feet while descending the bleachers. Once on the floor, I glanced back up at Grace, who winked and gave me a thumbs-up.

"Grace campaigned for you, not herself," Noah said, taking my hand. "She swore me to secrecy."

I stood with my brother, applause, hoots, and whistles washing over me, speechless with joyful tears running down my face.

It was the last moment of pure happiness I had that year.

CHAPTER ELEVEN

Spirit Week was a sequence of theme days, and Grace had made five outfits for me to wear. On Monday for school colors, she had me in a pencil-skirted plum suit with gold trim and buttons. Tuesday's retro day ensemble was from the eighties, an iridescent taffeta bubble skirt with an off-the-shoulder sequined top in gold.

I feared Wednesday's mascot day because hawthorn was the tree our school was named after. But Grace managed this by putting me in a purple t-shirt printed with the words March of the Ents and the image of a tree tearing a wall down.

On Thursday's pajama day, she gave me a golden satin nightgown with a purple lace dressing gown to go over it. Friday I was in my Bishop's Row uniform, with one addition: a Rocky Balboa-style robe with my number on the back.

"It should have been you," I said. "We both heard about Temperance last year, but you're the one who put together a plan. At the expense of your own happiness."

"Nah," she replied. "Everyone laughs at her now. Nobody will take her hatred seriously anymore. Finally, it feels like I can rest."

"Still. Wouldn't you rather show all these creations off by wearing them yourself?"

"My dream was always other people wearing them. I can get out of the spotlight, be myself," she said. "This was way harder than I thought it'd be."

After dinner, everyone headed to the gym again for a pep rally. Ezekiel and Nurse Smith teamed up at a DJ table to introduce the Bishop's Row teams. After that, the Monarchs would get their crowns on a platform under the scoreboard and the cheer squads would compete.

Peering out from the curtain in front of the locker room entrance, I spotted the Cheer Squad judges in the front row. Brianna tugged my sleeve, and we geeked out over a blonde woman in a powder-pink dress. She was Jeannie LaMontaigne, a Gallows Hill alumnus and member of the Tinfoil Hat pack from Providence Paranormal. Izzy's abuela sat out there too. She'd been a ballroom dance champ in her young adulthood. Azrael's oldest brother, a four-year dancer at the Boston Ballet, rounded out the judges.

We grouped by teams, waiting for our schools and numbers to be announced. Dylan elbowed me as they called Gallows Hill.

"Congratulations. Didn't get a chance to say it before."

"Thanks." I grinned.

"Must have been a near thing, competing with Grace's ego."

"That's not what happened," I told him.

"Oh." He blinked.

"You really thought she'd go low?"

"Didn't she? I mean, have you heard the rumors about Tempe?"

"Those didn't come from Grace."

"Huh." He shook his head. "Well, my mind's blown."

The voice on the PA called Messing Academy.

Tell him. If this isn't your moment, I don't know what is.

"Um. Maybe not yet."

"Please, Aliyah." He groaned. "Don't drop another devastating shoe. I can't handle it."

"No, no. This is a good thing. I hope."

"So say it."

"Dylan Khan." I took a breath as deep as the Atlantic Ocean. "For the last year and a half, I've had—"

The PA announcer boomed out, "Hawthorn Academy!"

And just like that, my moment evaporated.

I sat on the platform in the gym beside my brother, a heavy gilded crown on my head. The other four Monarchs did the same, with Cadence in front for her performance. An enormous banner hung behind us, emblazoned with the words Extramural Monarchs' Court. We watched as the Gallows Hill Cheer Squad took their places.

Born This Way by Lady Gaga boomed over the speakers and they launched into their routine, their energy breaching the stratosphere. The entire squad hugged afterward before returning to the bleachers. Cadence broke off to take her place beside Brianna afterward.

It took five minutes for Jacinda's squad to prepare since they had a set with screens to either side. The music started before they did.

"That's Portugal. The Man," Noah blinked. "Unconventional for cheering."

He called it. The Messing Squad's performance pushed the norm, from their entrance to the props. They leaped out from behind the screens, ribbons trailing from their wrists to the tune of *Feel it Still*. The routine combined dance styles and trappings from different eras and genres. It was totally unique and skillfully performed.

Hawthorn's squad went traditional, except for their music choice. Only Alex would have picked *Victorious* by Panic! At the Disco. Logan favored sure things and stability, and that showed in the classic cheerleading choreography. He'd made it a foundation for his performers to incorporate individual flourishes. The twins flung jazz hands everywhere. Grace executed splits and backflips in front of them. Alex and Logan tossed Kitty in the air like she weighed nothing, and their victory formation at the end built a tree instead of a pyramid with Arick at the top, augmented by Skinner the bookwyrm and Asceco the basilisk to represent branches.

After the tallies were in, Messing Academy won. All of the performances were so solid, it would have been a tough call if the judges had scored subjectively, but cheering had categories with numeric points. Jacinda's squad had scored ten points for creativity and also coordination, so they squeaked a win over Logan's by two points. Cadence's was only behind his by one, so they almost had a three-way tie.

The rally was over, and our coaches all wanted us to get plenty of rest before the games the next day. Most of the students and the others headed out into the halls. Many of the Bishop's Row players did too, but I noticed Noah and Jonah sneak away to the locker room.

Rat them out.

"No."

"Huh?" Cadence said. "Didn't catch that."

"Inside voice got out, sorry."

She threw her head back and laughed. I joined in, mostly to mask the sudden nervousness I felt. My friends had all gotten their chances to show off, put their talents out there, and be judged. Grace with her fashion, Izzy at the talent show, and Cadence here. Logan and Hal had had success at the Magipsych fair, and Noah had finally found someone to love who returned his feelings.

The next day would test my talents on the court against some of those same friends. That had to be the reason for my queasy stomach and shaky hands.

What if you're wrong?

"Hey, Aliyah!" Dylan flagged me down from the doors leading to the hall. "Smoothies?"

I sprinted after him. Maybe I'd get another moment after all.

The café was packed with Gallows Hill kids. I had to squeeze past what felt like an entire pack of wolf shifters before Bar spotted me and got them to make way.

"Royalty coming through!"

"Your Highness." One of them bowed.

"Oh, no. Just a joke," I insisted.

"If the troll's giving you fealty, I'm not gonna argue."

We laughed, and I finally made it to the counter. Dylan held a pair of banana berry smoothies, just like the one I'd had on the day I collapsed.

He said something, but I couldn't hear him. I beckoned him into the corner Noah had sat in with Jonah on the first day I'd seen them together, figuring a little good luck couldn't hurt. He leaned over the small round table, close enough for me to hear.

"What did you want to say? Back in the locker room, I mean?"

The bottom dropped out of my courage. I took a sip of the smoothie, closing my eyes in an attempt to calm myself, and it back-fired as spectacularly as July Fourth firework because that magic sight ability kicked in. Behind my eyelids, I saw Noah and Jonah cowering in fear someplace with tiles, and somehow there was fire and rain.

Go back to the gym. Now.

"I'm sorry. I've got to go." I stood up, leaving both Dylan and the smoothie behind and prepared to fight my way back through the crowd.

Cadence saw.

"Everybody move!"

Her voice created a path and I took it immediately, lifting knees and elbows to sprint away at top speed. Noah would probably laugh in my face or get angry if I interrupted an epic makeout session.

I didn't care.

If he was in trouble and I didn't barge in, I'd never forgive myself. I'd do anything to stop my brother from getting hurt, a fact made clear on my first day at Hawthorn when I threatened the third-year's It Girl to defend his integrity.

I'd save his life alone if I had to, but as I ran, I felt someone behind me—a powerful presence.

I glanced over my shoulder to find Ember flapping madly to keep up with me. Nobody else was there.

You're never alone.

"You're. Not. Real," I panted.

I couldn't be haunted. Ghosts couldn't manifest on the Hawthorn campus, but the feeling persisted. I continued on, holding my hands out to fling open the academic wing's doors.

For a moment, I worried about breaking the stained glass mural crafted by Hal's grandmother, but it held even under my panic-induced motions.

As I ran down the hall to the gym, my body responded perfectly to my demands on it like I was made for this specific action at this particular moment.

Coincidence is on your side. Don't squander it.

The gym was dark. The platform with the Monarchs' seats was still standing, but the banner was missing. Someone stood by the bleachers, a tall and lanky figure that froze as I passed. I had no time for whoever it was. My gut felt like lead, but my arms and legs only moved faster toward the locker room.

Inside, I skidded to a stop in the common space. A shower was running, but I couldn't tell where it was over the sound of my ragged gasps for air. One glance at the floor told me I needed the gender-neutral section. A scrap of purple and gold fabric lay by the doorway, emblazoned with a two—Noah's jersey number.

I paced ahead, stepping softly and slowly. Whoever had orchestrated my brother's distress didn't deserve the courtesy of a warning. Ember landed on my shoulder, clinging to it like a life raft in a stormy sea.

It was Temperance, of course, and her behavior defied the meaning of her name. She held the Axis device I'd only seen on paper in front of her, pointing it at my brother and Jonah, who sat under one of the showerheads, soaked to the bone.

Above them hung the banner that had recently been in the gym. She'd changed the words to read Least Likely to Succeed.

And I smelled blood.

CHAPTER TWELVE

Blood Like Water
Temperance

Their meddling had made me sick, from the first day when DuBois upstaged me to winter break when Dylan Khan refused to step into my parlor like a good little fly. What had me steamed was that talebearing coward, Spanos. I knew he'd been behind the gnome rumor, which was infuriating.

The sissy ice magus wouldn't escape my wrath. He and that trash gryphon were getting boiled away as soon as I had the chance.

I had other prey to stalk first, a parentally imposed duty that now fell to me. Charity was weak, refused to get her hands dirty, and Faith had gone off the rails, siding with the inferiors. I'd always known exterminating parasites was my destiny. More than that, it was my calling in life, according to my parents.

Why else had they given me this marvelous toy?

I hid with Precious in the shadows behind the bleachers, watching the leech hold hands with his favorite blood bag. It was disgusting how vampires carried on with living people. You didn't fall in love with a cheeseburger. Leeches were lying vermin, incapable of love, mocking life. People like Noah Morgenstern were worse, making it look normal to date predators.

Samuel Ives and I hadn't been anything like that, of course. We were pure magi, no weak psychics, savage shifters, or Unseelie faeries in our heritage. We'd made a natural match until someone ratted us out. I wasn't sure who, but that was the only explanation for Faith's hissy fit after the Magipsych Fair.

After that, I deliberately dropped hints at the most biased faculty member. Susan DeBeer had gone to undergrad with my mother, so I knew all about how her advisor, an extramagus with poison and mind magic, had taken advantage of her. Luciano was supposed to take the fall in her "inappropriate behavior" witch hunt and get blamed for poisoning Clementine and Seth.

Aliyah Morgenstern had cleared him and doomed my relationship. Samuel broke up with me at the end of January and resigned the next day. I'd lost my boyfriend, so now she'd lose a brother. If I did everything perfectly, nobody would suspect me, either.

"Go in the locker room already," I murmured, rolling my eyes.

Precious caressed my cheek with one cold webbed hand. I'd be patient like him. He hadn't gotten up to any mischief since exacting my revenge on Bailey Overton for defecting to the inferiors.

Finally, they went in, laughing, with their arms around each other. I took my time unfastening the banner and making modifications to it by wetting the ink and moving it around. I checked my bag for my secret weapon, ensuring it was fully charged with every magical element I'd need so nobody could pin this on me. If we struck too early, the vermin could escape. Besides, I wanted everything to be perfect for my first act of righteous justice.

The altered sign would make as much of a statement as the pile of ashes and the dead snake. Noah's familiar would be collateral damage.

I sent Precious in first. He got into the pipes through the drain in the steam room, using the water inside to locate the leech and his supper. They were in the gender-neutral showers with the water off. As I snuck in, Precious opened the pipes, covering them with enough water to give me the upper hand.

The undead thing took a step toward me.

"Freeze, leech!" I twirled my hand, twisting water around his feet, giving it maximum cohesion and immobilizing him.

"What the f—" I swung a punch, my magic calling water to slap Noah across the face.

"On your knees, both of you." I pulled out the device my parents had given me. "Or you both die. This makes me an extramagus. Don't make me demonstrate it."

Precious took off, dashing after something scaly that slithered across the floor. I couldn't look away from the vermin in front of me, but I checked Morgenstern's shoulder. His familiar still clung there, though his uniform had torn and was hanging askew.

The leech mumbled something about time.

"Did I say you could talk?"

"No." Noah snorted. "Fine, we're getting down. Come on, Jonah. We can pretend we're on a picnic. In a rainstorm."

"That's right, but only the leech is getting anything to eat. He's turning you, Morgenstern."

"No." The vamp kneeled but shook his head. "I won't take away his choice."

I held one hand up, drawing water out of the air around it until I had enough to drown a man. I flung it at Morgenstern, pushing it down his nose and throat.

"Turn him or he dies."

Noah's eyes bulged, and he clawed at his throat in vain. I almost thought the leech wouldn't go through with it, but he caved when Noah toppled over. I called the water back, not wanting to kill Morgenstern too soon.

My lip curled into a sneer as I watched the leech drink. It was every bit as nasty as I'd imagined, and the fact that I'd forced them into it had my heart racing. I chortled, finally victorious, owning the undesirables.

Until that leech raised his eyebrow at me because of course, his unnatural hearing let him hear my heartbeat.

"Stop." I splashed the coldest water I could find at them.

"I'm sorry," the vermin said, but not to me.

"It's okay," Morgenstern croaked, tears running down his face. "I forgive you."

"Now drink from the leech, Morgenstern."

"Noah, don't." The leech's eyes filled with what could only be crocodile tears.

"Listen up, parasite." I patted my device. "I'm giving you ten seconds to say farewell to Morgenstern's humanity. If he's not vamped by then, I'm frying both of you."

I punctuated that long goodbye with my voice, counting their last moments down.

CHAPTER THIRTEEN

Aliyah

I stood transfixed by the scene before me, frozen in time and space as Temperance spoke.

"Time's up. Any last words?"

"Go hump a gnome." Noah rolled his eyes.

"Lies!" she screamed. "Fake news!"

"Protest much, Gertrude?" My brother was a master of sass and awe. "Wait. Hamlet's mom didn't get nasty with gnomes."

"You took everything from me," she snarled. "Now drink!"

"Please don't." Jonah sobbed. "Let him go. Just kill me instead."

"Shut up, leech!" She stamped her foot, splashing in maybe six inches of water. "You both die."

I stepped forward.

"You have to get through me first."

Temperance turned her head, took one look at me, and sneered.

"Grace's pet extramagus? Fire and sunlight, all out of control. Try taking me down without killing them both in the process. I dare you."

"Okay." I held my hands in conjuring position, stepping closer to Noah and Jonah. "Ember!"

My dragonet reared up, letting out a throaty roar as she mingled her magic with mine. I took a deep breath, preparing to superheat her weapon so she'd drop it, but Ember's roar turned into a yawn, and she sat back on her haunches.

She drained your familiar just now.

Tempe pointed the device at me. As she pulled the trigger, I experienced an all-too-familiar feeling.

"Poison?" My legs wavered. "Is that all you've got?"

I turned my fire inward, sending it through my veins and burning the toxin out of my blood. I resumed my stance, inching forward to put more of my body between the device and the boys. Jonah tried to push Noah toward the door.

"Precious!" Temperance called. "Make sure he's turned!"

The grundylow emerged from a drain in a disturbing fashion, squeezing up through the holes to head Noah off. Precious leaped at my brother's bloodstained neck with his webbed hands outstretched.

A cry pierced the air, and a streak of white feathers and fur flashed toward the grundylow in mid-leap, knocking him aside.

Precious hissed, retreating under the shower spray. Mercy the gryphon circled, trapping him in the corner.

"Aliyah!" Dorian called from the doorway. He wheezed, and the water in the air made his shirt cling to something under it in the front. "Run defense!"

"You lying bitch!" Temperance pointed the device at Dorian.

Mercy's wings stopped flapping and she dropped out of the air, hitting the wet tile with a sickening smack.

Dorian's eyes widened and his lip trembled, but he conjured ice anyway, trying to block her attack. It melted because she'd shot him with a copy of my fire. The resulting water knocked him face-down in the puddle, the remainder of the flames burned away the back of his hair and shirt, revealing a binder.

Everything seemed to happen at once, like when I freed Alex at the dance. Tempe's device let out another blast of flame, at my brother this time. Precious thrust Jonah's bloodied wrist into Noah's mouth. Mercy's wing flapped once, weakly. Temperance raised her free hand, then punched down, flattening the gryphon with a watery hammer.

"Murderer!" I pointed at her.

"Pest control." Tempe narrowed her eyes. "And I'm not done yet."

I'd never seen a vampire Rage and had no idea how primal a force they channeled.

Jonah tore free of Precious's grasp, flinging the grundylow away. His eyes glowed a baleful red, his bared fangs sharp and long. He crouched, hissing, prepared to pounce.

I leaped in front of Jonah, expecting her to use the device to incinerate him. I held my hands out, a small orb with both my elements in front of me.

Bishop's Row was the closest thing I knew to battle tactics. My defensive play might have worked, but Temperance had watched me all year. She knew my biggest weakness on the court—the classic fakeout.

She aimed at Noah instead. He should have perished on the spot because even Jonah's vampiric dash back to his side wasn't as fast as lightning, but he didn't die.

The bolt hit him, fanning out along the water. The lightning paralyzed him and it had the same effect on Jonah, so he was turned.

Water arced over Tempe's head, forming what looked like a Faraday cage, but its deadly bolt continued toward Dorian and me.

Ice crashed through the room in a shimmering glacial wall and the lightning shattered it. My hair crackled and stood on end, but it absorbed enough of the charge to save us.

The ice was purple like in the mural, but nobody had conjured that since my great-uncle's time here with Filberto Luciano.

Bert became an extramagus when he fell in love, and his powers had reverted once Noah the elder died. That's what's in his sealed record.

"Stop, Miss Fairbanks." Professor Luciano stepped forward, shaking purple ice off his fingers. "I won't let you hurt them."

She laughed.

"Look at them." She smirked. "Slavering monsters. I'm defending myself."

"We're all witnesses. You'll go to prison." He held out his hand. "It's not too late to do the right thing, Tempe. Let me help you. Give me the device."

"If I kill you all, I write this story and win my family's legacy." Her grin was sharp and painful. "I've got all the power here. You just want to steal it."

"Love is my power." He stepped beside me. "My love for this school and everyone in it is a strength beyond your imagination. You will do no more harm. Miss Morgenstern, get them to safety."

I wanted to defy his orders and make this stand with him because nobody should have to fight evil alone, but Noah gasped and Dorian groaned. They needed me more.

The heat and light had driven Jonah to the brink, and his closest, most vulnerable target was Dorian.

Noah wasted no time. He squinted, wincing at the solar flares in his hands, but managed to keep Jonah at bay.

I dashed for Dorian, grabbing him under the arms and dragging him into the common room before going back in.

Tempe blasted Noah's hands with more solar energy, overloading him. If I couldn't help him banish it, we'd all get incinerated.

Jonah's hands were on fire, and he wasn't in the shower spray any longer. He shrieked, the Rage transforming into a flight response. I could see the bones in his fingers.

Professor Luciano pulled ice from the floor and encased Jonah's hands, dousing the blaze. The injured vampire dashed into the dark cave of the changing area. I hurried to my brother's side.

"Aliyah, get out." He sobbed, staring at the twin suns in his hands. "I can't banish it. I'm going to kill everyone."

"We'll stop it together." I stared at his eyes. "Look at me."

I knelt beside him and took his hands, using the same banishing technique Elanor had taught me. He finally met my gaze, nodding. I took a deep breath and remembered every time we'd saved each other in much smaller ways. They flashed through the blinding light between us in an instant.

The night I was sure the Kraken hid under my bed, and he let me sleep in his room.

The day he came home from middle school friendless, and I said I'd always love him.

The Sukkot he'd shared his sleeping bag so I'd be brave enough to sleep outside all night.

The Passover he came out as gay, and I was the first one to hug him.

The day he helped me pack for my first year at Hawthorn.

"I love you, Noah. No matter what."

"Forever, Aliyah."

That was supposed to be our goodbye to each other and the world because all that effort wasn't enough. This amount of energy was impossible for us to banish on our own.

Through the light, I saw a feathery shadow diving. It flew at Tempe's face, and she flung her hands up to fend off the strix's poisoned claws. The professor lunged forward, grabbing the device. He clutched it to his chest, then turned his head to look at me.

"Professor, no." My eyes widened. "It drains life."

"I choose whose."

Professor Luciano pointed the device at the impossible globe of light. He staggered, knees splashing on ice, water, and tile. He pulled the trigger with one hand and clutched his heart with the other.

I gripped my brother's hands tighter, still contributing my effort to banish what felt like the sun. The light diminished, damping back down to normal levels for the human eye. Noah's hands were colder than a winter ocean. A stain darkened the front of his jersey, red rimmed his eyes, and blood caked his lips. He wasn't breathing.

We locked gazes, me and my brother the vampire.

Temperance lay on the floor with her eyes open, a single shallow scratch on her cheek. I could tell by the way her chest rose and fell and how Precious held her head between his webbed hands that she was paralyzed.

Professor Luciano curled motionless, still clutching the Axis device. His strix hopped toward him, waterlogged feathers temporarily grounding her. She preened a tuft of hair behind his ear, then let out three mournful hoots.

Ember swooped off my shoulder, landing beside the professor's familiar. She keened, as she had on the day we all thought Doris had died.

"No."

My brother ran toward the door. I rushed to the professor's side. There had to be hope. I pulled his shoulder, turning him from his side to his back, and he opened his eyes.

"Thank you." His hand remained on his chest over his heart.

"I got you hurt." I sniffled, my face wetter than it had been. "Bad."

"Badly," he corrected with a final raised eyebrow. "I banished the sun to spare all of you."

Noah returned. "Hold on. Help is coming."

"Stay with me, Bert." I pulled his hands away from the device, wrapping mine around them, but they were almost as cold as Noah's.

"We all die, but love doesn't." He gasped. "Keep fighting. Heed the magic. Its tone is harsh but never wrong."

"Is that the voice I hear in my head?"

He glanced down at my *Shema Yisrael* pendant, then back at my face. He smiled, somehow looking through me as though he'd just recognized an old friend.

Professor Filberto Luciano had no more answers for me or anyone else in this world.

He'd left it.

CHAPTER FOURTEEN

Pulling the purple and gold robe off, I used it to cover Professor Luciano's head and shoulders.

Some part of me would never stop shaking and crying, even after the physical feelings had passed. That sorrow felt vast and eternal, just like love. Maybe that was why it loomed so large, because grief is the space our loved ones leave behind.

Turning to Noah didn't come close to filling it, but it helped. We embraced, leaning together in the dank shower's relative quiet.

"Peep." Ember nestled against me, curling her tail around my shoulders.

"Hiss." Lotan slithered away from him and on to my shoulder with Ember, though I couldn't fathom why. She'd always comforted him through sadness before. Noah clung more tightly to me, sobbing harder. I hoped she was just cold, not rejecting him.

A quartet of adults arrived, but I only noticed one at first. I was mesmerized by Stephanie Hawkins saving Jonah Arnold, something only a dhampyr could do. She deliberately cut her wrist and used it to coax Jonah out of the changing room and down from his Rage. He reached up, pulling the arm close and covering it with his lips.

All the polish and poise, the wide-eyed cheer and positivity about her person vanished as though her ex-husband had transported it away with space magic. Mrs. Hawkins was exactly as dour as Hal had described. As Jonah drank from her, flesh knitted over the charred bone of his fingertips and the blisters on his face faded. Stephanie sobbed, eyes focused on something or someone not here.

She must have been a blood doll.

"Hold me back." Noah lunged, so I caught him.

Like before, he felt colder than he should have, but the biggest difference between now and then was a drastic increase in strength. No matter how hard I held on, I couldn't fight him. Not even with all the extra training. My grip slipped and he dashed toward Stephanie, fangs out. Somewhere behind me, a dog barked.

"Hold!" Faith called behind me.

My brother froze in place, jaw dropped, bicuspids impossibly long.

"March." She stepped into view, holding her hand out to Noah, who followed her command.

The air shimmered between them, but I knew better. I was watching undeath magic at work. She continued, accompanying him until they both got out of the room.

"You murdered my colleague." Professor DeBeer glared. "And this poor gryphon. Do you have anything to say for yourself?"

Temperance held her hands in front of her, bound by a set of black metal cuffs. Precious muttered glumly inside what looked like a fishbowl with a lid made of the same black metal.

"I should have thought bigger. Exterminated the inferiors, not just the vermin who infected them."

Professor DeBeer sniffed. "I hope they throw the book at you."

"You would have taken the fall." Tempe giggled. "The way you carry on about extramagi, you sound almost exactly like them."

"Keep talking if you want," Azrael's aunt from Salem PD said from the doorway, "but you have the right to remain silent."

Kim Ichiro stepped out from behind her with a contingent of local MCSIs.

The squeak of a knob turning caught my attention. Headmaster Hawkins stood by the shower's control with a blue nitrile glove on his hand and turned it off, his face covered with water, dark and still like welder's glass. Whether it was from the spray or tears, I couldn't tell. He reached down, touching Jonah's head. Stephanie put her free hand on his arm. He snapped his fingers, and they all vanished.

"Poor Dorian." Nurse Smith shook his head. I watched his back as he bent down, scooping the gryphon up.

"Mercy?" I asked.

"She's gone." He turned, revealing the tears on his face. "Are you the one who moved him?"

I nodded, unable to speak past the lump in my throat.

"Probably saved his life. He could have drowned face down in this water."

I couldn't hold myself together anymore and collapsed to the floor, ears ringing. Somewhere in the distance, a woman sobbed. When I took a breath, it paused. *I* was making that noise.

The karkinos crawled out of Nurse Smith's pocket and enlarged, then lifted me to his back. The rocking motion of his stride was the last thing I remembered before passing out.

I woke in my room instead of the infirmary. Oddly, I felt good, until the memory of what had happened crashed like a wave against my consciousness.

My eyes stung as I went through motions. Get the bathroom bag. Put on the robe. Walk to the restroom. Brush teeth, wash face, shower. Back to the room to dress, not paying attention to which clothes go on the body. Open the door again.

"Aliyah?" Elanor stood in the hall, her uniform on, including ankyr, ballistae, and cestus. "I brought a spare uniform. Whistle's in a half hour. Are you going to make it?"

"Is Noah?"

"He can't." She shook her head.

"I'll make it. For him."

"Are you sure?"

"If it were Logan, what would you say?"

"Same thing."

After changing, I followed her down the hall, the stairs, through the lobby. Faith joined us, also wearing her uniform and walking over from the café.

"Drink this." Faith handed me a smoothie, then took a swig from her cup.

"Not banana berry."

Noah will never drink banana berry smoothies again.

"No. Green tea and coconut."

"Good. Thanks." I slugged it down so fast I got an ice cream headache.

We pushed through the doors to the academic wing. *Long Division.* The mural held a different meaning for me now, just like its counterpart, *Fire and Ice.* Together and separate. Opposite and intimate. Contributions from students like us, two generations ago by people learning in the same halls. Maybe we didn't have to repeat their mistakes.

"Where's everyone else?"

"Either the locker room or the bleachers," Elanor answered. "You remember who we're playing?"

"Messing." I nodded. "Gallows Hill after."

"Just checking." She held her hands against the gym's doors. "You ready?"

"Just a sec." I went to pull my hair back but realized I didn't have an elastic.

"Here." Faith handed me a familiar-looking one.

"Thanks for letting me borrow—"

"That's your lucky one, remember? I'm returning it. Now put your hair up, and let's go."

I did. We went.

Izzy played reverse point instead of Jonah, who remained in the infirmary with my brother. I'd taken Noah's place as first defense, with Faith off reserves at my usual mid position. Before the starting whistle, Dylan glanced at me. He said nothing, but the puffy redness around his eyes spoke volumes. We shared this grief.

"For Noah," I said.

He nodded.

Elanor did the coin toss with Izzy, and Messing got first throw.

The cestus the psychics wore gave their orbs colors. On the surface, the gameplay looked the same, but it felt totally different for one major reason: none of the psychic energy mingled with our elemental magic. That meant we couldn't absorb orbs. They either bounced off or canceled each other out.

That was how it had always worked for the Messing kids, who seemed used to it. We suffered due to the learning curve. A psychic orb bounced off Dylan's ice defense, tagging Faith out on the first throw, but after that, we didn't repeat the mistake. All the same, we lost the first match against Messing.

Fortunately, today was best two out of three. We won the second match quickly but by the skin of our teeth, still adapting to the gameplay difference. It was a real nail-biter, with just Izzy and Elanor left at the end.

The third game went much longer. Faith hung in for a long time, undeath magic enhancing her endurance, but in the end she went out, taking their second defense with her. Messing still had four players, with their remaining mid left recharging her orb. Only Dylan, Elanor, and I remained on our side. It looked bleak. As soon as Izzy finished her conjure, we'd be toast unless we played perfectly.

Messing's last salvo before Elanor's final gambit was a trio of orbs thrown at the same time. I got tagged out leaping into the air to absorb two with my body and left the last for Dylan, the only way for two defense to counter three throws at once.

That was a move Noah would be proud of.

"Thanks."

"You're welcome?" Messing's first defense blinked.

The buzzer sounded. Izzy was out, tagged by Elanor's throw. We'd won.

Everything else about our victory went by in a blur of purple and gold. I only remember the roar of the crowd, a sense of being carried, and Elanor's face: a smile on lips under tear-streaked eyes, embracing Coach Pickman.

All of us celebrated and mourned at the same time in some way. Dylan alone, howling with his face turned heavenward. Lee off the bench, leaning on Izzy's shoulders, the green and orange of her uniform clashing with his. Faith sobbing openly, her arm linked with mine. My eyes had no more tears, so I cried on the inside.

Like everything else for me that day, the victory was hollow. In the locker room, that same sense of futile routine motion took over. Shower, dry, change. Head out. I avoided looking in the direction of the gender-neutral area, but a flutter of yellow caught my eye there.

"Police line, do not cross." I read.

"Come on, Aliyah." Dylan linked hands with me. "You don't need to be here."

He led me back out into the now-empty gym.

"I've had a crush on you." I blurted. "For ages."

"I'm gay."

We stopped, let go, and stared at each other. I blinked first.

"But Grace?"

"That was awkward because I loved her, but physically, nothing was there."

"I get it." I nodded. "You can be in love without sex."

"I'm surprised you understand."

"It's the way I feel about you."

"Aliyah." He shook his head. "You're like a sister."

"I'll live." I nodded. "I'm going to the infirmary. Come with me?"

"Sure."

We stopped at the cafe for sandwiches, got them to go, and headed down.

The only other person in the room with Noah was Dorian, who slept on his side, hooked up to some kind of beeping machine.

Professor Luciano's strix perched on the headboard, head under her wing. A white box sat on his bedside table, surrounded by flowers. I'd seen one of those every time Bubbe lost a patient. Mercy was inside. Her earthly remains, anyway.

"Where's Jonah?" I blinked back tears. "Didn't Stephanie save him?"

"Salem Jail." Noah sighed. "They arrested him because of my new sun allergy."

"Tempe forced you!" Dylan slammed his hand on the bedside table. "Don't they make exceptions for that here?"

"Did." I leaned back in my chair. "During and right after the Reveal, but those days are long gone, and the laws changed."

"Jonah's stuck unless Tempe's convicted of coercing him. You need a permit ahead of time and clear consent with witnesses when it happens." Noah picked at the edge of his blanket. "Believe me, I checked. Recently."

"What about you?" Dylan asked. "Will they let you out in time for the game tomorrow?"

"They're giving me blood every half hour. New vamps need that until their bodies adjust to being undead." He sighed. "It usually takes twenty-four hours, but even when I'm out, I can't play."

"Why not?"

"I have to leave Hawthorn." He closed his eyes. "No vampire students allowed. The only reason I'm still on campus is that it's dangerous to move me for at least the next eight hours."

"Headmaster Hawkins wouldn't kick you out."

"He didn't." Alex Onassis walked through the door, holding a bouquet of lilies. "The Board of Trustees makes the rules for admission. All the headmaster decides on his own is faculty, staff, and events. The board's meeting after the game with Gallows Hill. They might vote to replace him."

"What are you doing here?" Noah's eyes gleamed red.

"These are for Dorian." He crossed the room, placing the flowers in a jar at Dorian's bedside. "I was about to head in there last night. He stopped me and sent me to get a professor because I could run faster."

"It would have been me in that bed." Alex turned his back on us and sniffled before continuing, "Asceco in that box. I owe Dorian Spanos an enormous debt, so leave me alone, Noah."

"He saved us too, then." I sniffled. "Because Professor Luciano wouldn't have gotten there in time without either of them."

"And I called him selfish." Dylan hung his head. "Lazy. A coward."

"Jerk," Dorian croaked.

"What?" Dylan looked up.

Dorian reached for water but missed. Alex got it for him. After taking a sip, he spoke again.

"You forgot 'jerk.'"

"Yeah, I did." Dylan looked up. "And I'm sorry. It was easier to blame you for my problems instead of dealing with them."

"Dorian, I'm so sorry." I stood, clenching my fists. "You might not know it yet—"

"Mercy's gone." He closed his eyes, cradling the water glass in his hands. "The headmaster told me last night."

"Oh. Thought you just woke up."

"Nah."

"What's the beepy thing for then?" Dylan asked.

"Heart monitor." Dorian opened his eyes. "It stopped."

"Dude." Dylan blinked.

"I was dead for like thirty seconds."

Everyone sniffled, noses and faces wet—even Alex.

"Guys, it's okay." One corner of his mouth turned up. "Nobody can beat me in the goth cred department now."

"You're taking all this extremely well." Noah raised an eyebrow.

"No. With snark is how I take everything." He set the glass down. "But mostly, it's because your grandma visited this morning for over an hour while they fed Noah in the other room."

"Ah." I nodded.

"Now, if you all wouldn't mind keeping it down, me and my resuscitated ticker need more rest." He jerked a thumb at the strix on the headboard. "And the weird owl, too."

Noah shooed us out, insisting he was just getting to the good part in the latest installment of his favorite space opera series. We left our friends in whatever peace they could salvage.

We played Gallows Hill the next day, trouncing them rapidly in two matches. I'm not sure whether we had more ferocity because of Noah's being kicked out or if Brianna's team just didn't have the heart to compete after all the tragedy.

Azrael was especially off his game, which wasn't surprising when I thought about it later. He'd grown up idolizing Noah and had been excited about competing against him on the court. Without that aspect, he lost focus.

After the final whistle, Brianna rushed over and hugged each of us in turn instead of the usual post-game series of handshakes. All of the other Gallows Hill players followed suit, even Crow, who swallowed his bad-boy demeanor for once. At the end of the line, when I came to Bar, he lifted me off the ground.

"Your friends, your brother, and your professor deserved better than what they got. I'm sorry, Aliyah." He put me back down.

As the crowd dispersed, that hollow feeling returned, but Logan came over and stood by my side.

"Whatever happens, I'm here."

He took my hand and squeezed, gaze on the floor away from my face. Eye contact wasn't the same for him as other people, but that little hand squeeze was worth a thousand intensely cinematic gazes. It gave me just as much comfort as hugging Noah back in the locker room in the wake of all that tragedy.

"Thanks, Logan." I squeezed back. "For everything."

I could end by telling you that Grace got hired on all summer at Ambersmith Fashions, or that Logan got an internship at Bubbe's office.

Or that Elanor Pierce rented a basement apartment in the Point with Noah before the ink on her diploma was dry.

But I won't. None of those had the same impact on my year as the first day back on Monday morning, when life at Hawthorn went on without Noah, Mercy, and Professor Luciano.

It started with a special announcement before breakfast by Headmaster Hawkins in the lobby. He stood at the podium, waving us toward the rows of chairs as we descended the stairs. Once everyone was seated, he spoke.

"First, it is with great sorrow that I officially announce the passing of Professor Luciano, who graced us with his wisdom and guidance. He lost his life heroically, banishing a magical threat that could have caused mass casualties on campus. During this effort, Mercy, the gryphon familiar of Mr. Dorian Spanos, also perished. They will be sorely missed."

Headmaster Hawkins clapped his hands, activating the magipsychic display behind him. Pictures of Mercy and Professor Luciano appeared, with the words In Memoriam between them.

"As a direct consequence of this tragedy, Mr. Noah Morgenstern has been deemed ineligible to continue attending classes. The nature of his condition is private at his own request. A student was responsible for this deliberate threat to our campus. Temperance Fairbanks was expelled and turned over to the Federal Bureau of Extrahumans, where her actions and motives will be investigated and prosecuted in accordance with national law."

He cleared his throat before continuing.

"The Board of Trustees held an emergency meeting last night. I am instructing section one of the second-year cohort for the remainder of this semester in addition to my other duties. That said, I'll be stepping out of the headmaster's role at the end of this academic year, remaining to serve as a professor to that same group of students next fall."

He raised his hand, quelling the voices that rose in protest.

"The Board of Trustees voted to demote me but keep me on. They were generous, and the paperwork is already signed. A letter will go out this summer with the name of the new headmaster, selected from a list of candidates I have compiled for them. I will forever be honored by each and every one of my students. Thank you."

After the meeting, we sat together in the biggest booth over breakfast.

"Trustees?" Grace wrinkled her nose. "Doesn't that include one of Faith's parents?"

"Yeah, my father." Faith opened her mouth and mimed sticking her finger down her throat.

"Mine too," Logan added.

"And Mrs. Onassis." Hailey wrinkled her nose.

"There are four more, you know." Bailey stirred her coffee.

"That's why my dad's still teaching. Miss Dunstable and Mr. Thurston are his godparents, and Mr. Gauthier went to college with him."

"What about trustee number seven?" Dorian asked.

"I don't know him, but he's an undeath magus from upstate New York." Hal sighed. "I overheard Dad say he voted to spite Mr. Fairbanks. They don't get along."

The string of words out of Faith's mouth made everyone stop and stare.

"What?" I asked.

"Temperance. I bet she was under orders."

"Isn't that kind of paranoid?" Kitty tossed her head.

"No." Faith and Logan answered in chorus.

"This spells trouble next year for sure." I leaned my chin on my hand. "What if the new headmaster is Mrs. Pierce or something? No offense, Logan."

"That won't happen." Hal tapped his temple. "Dad's smart. One of his terms for resignation was the list he mentioned. It says that any new headmaster must be one of the people on that list. We won't know what we're dealing with until the board chooses, though."

"For now, let's just try to get through the week, okay?" Lee said. "And actually eat our breakfasts." It was good advice, so we took it.

I wondered whether the headmaster would give us a reading

assignment in the library or send us to Creatives, but neither happened. He taught us as promised, but did nothing as tone-deaf or heartless as attempting to take Filberto Luciano's place.

He assigned us to make our own tribute as a class to our mentor and to Mercy. Logan sketched them both from memory, adding Mercy to his right shoulder instead of his strix. Faith made paper cranes, passing them around for everyone to decorate. Dylan wrote poems about courage and lost love, then dragged out his guitar and set them to music. Hal asked me what the professor's last words were, then wrote them out on parchment with calligraphic ink, adding his thumbprint as punctuation at the end.

Dorian didn't have the heart to do much besides watch. I overheard the headmaster telling him about the academic track. My classmate walked to the front of the room, his head held high, and announced that he'd be back to graduate with us next year, no matter what. We each went over and hugged him. Yes, even Dylan.

At the last minute before the bell, the strix woke and swooped down from a rafter. She landed on the desk, hooting at the other familiars, and they assembled in a semicircle on the floor, howling, keening, caterwauling, and squeaking in their own mourning ritual, aimed at Dorian. For Mercy. Logan stood beside me, weeping. When the critters stopped, the strix hooted at Logan, then blinked at Dorian, hopping toward him.

"What?"

"She's offering you her sympathies," Logan said. "And her name is Julia."

"Thanks, Julia." Dorian held out his hand. "My condolences. He was the best teacher I ever had. You must miss him terribly."

She tapped his hand with her beak, then peered at him and hooted.

"Yeah, sure, if you don't mind the gym." He held out his arm, but Julia fluttered to his shoulder. "It kinda reeks in there, but you know that already."

"I think they'll be okay, Logan." I patted his arm. "Thanks to you."

He nodded, wiping away tears.

Before we left, the door to Professor Luciano's classroom was covered from top to bottom with our handiwork. Finally, I added my own tribute: a single white feather and an envelope postmarked Genoa, Italy 1982, to Noah Morgenstern at 10-1/2 Hawthorne Street, Salem, Massachusetts. I'd keep the letter, but the envelope on the door would always be filled with love.

The story continues with book Seven, *Mind of Distinction*, coming soon to Amazon and Kindle Unlimited

GLOSSARY

People

- **Changeling**- A mortal child of either one or two faerie parents. Most changelings choose a monarch sometime in their twenties, although some do it earlier than they have to.
- **Dampyr**- The mortal offspring of two vampires. They aren't as rare as many suspect, although because their blood is exceptionally sustaining to vampires, they keep their status secret. Dampyr sometimes have magic or psychic powers that work unreliably.
- **Faerie**- A term used to describe either a changeling who has tithed to a monarch and spent a year and a day in the Under or the pure creatures such as Gnomes and Pixies who were created by the king and queen.
- **Ghost**- A dead person with unfinished business becomes a ghost. If a mortal makes a contract before death, that gives them unfinished business and lets them linger. When ghosts finish their business, they move on, but no one knows where they go from here.
- **Magus**- A mortal who can use magic. Magic comes from

energy in the world. Most magi can only use one type of magic. However, a rare few can do more than one kind. Those are called extramagi.

- **Merfolk**- People who can live on land with legs or in the sea with fins and tails. They only emerged from the ocean after the Big Reveal and are still extremely rare outside of harbor towns.
- **Psychic**- A mortal with psychic power. Psychic ability comes from a person's own body and mind.
- **Vampire**- An unliving person who drinks blood to survive and enhance their abilities. Only regular mortals, psychics, and magi can get turned into vampires. Shifters, changelings, and faeries won't turn, and most of those won't survive an attempt.
- **Shifter**- A mortal who can take an animal's shape. Shifters have one form, with coloring similar to what they have while human. They usually have an enhanced sense while human-shaped, which goes along with their animal. For example, an owl shifter might have keen eyesight and a wolf shifter, a great sense of smell.

Shifter Varieties

- **Dragon**- The only shifters who can see both magic and psychic abilities, though only while shifted. The most powerful ones can partially shapeshift. Dragons are immortal and reproduce infrequently. There are so few of them since the Reveal that they've started taking other magical shifters as mates.
- **Kelpie**- A magical shifter who gets their abilities from an enchanted faerie pelt that bonds with their soul. The Kelpie pelts were created by the Goblin King, so they have Unseelie energy and restrictions. A Kelpie's animal form is a horse. Families pass the pelts down through generations,

and part of each ancestor lives on to help their descendants. The ancestors can get distracting, however.

- **Selkie**- A magical shifter who gets their abilities from an enchanted faerie pelt that bonds with their soul. The Selkie pelts were created by the Sidhe queen, so they have Seelie energy and restrictions. A Selkie's animal form is a seal or sometimes a sea otter. They can use water magic as long as they wear the pelt. Families pass the pelts down through the generations, and part of each ancestor lives on to help their descendants. The ancestors can get distracting, however.
- **Tanuki**- A magical shifter with enhanced speed and the ability to see all types of magic while shifted. They are also the only creatures who can manipulate luck, causing it to turn from good to bad or the other way around. They stop aging if they own a charm infused with luck from humans. Very few of those charms exist, having been either used up during the Reveal or locked away.

Powers

- **Air magic**- The power to conjure, control, and banish wind or air.
- **Earth magic**- The power to conjure, control, and banish earth, sand, or rock.
- **Empathy**- A psychic power to sense and influence emotions in other people.
- **Fire magic**- The power to conjure, control, and banish flames.
- **Ice magic**- The power to conjure, control, and banish ice.
- **Lightning magic**- The power to conjure, control, and banish lightning.
- **Poison magic**- The power to conjure, control, and banish poison. Each magus has a slightly different type of toxin they produce. Some are even antidotes to others.
- **Precognitive**- A psychic power to foretell future events.

- **Spectral magic**- the power to conjure, control, and banish light.
- **Spectral Affinity**- A trait some spectral magi have that makes them charismatic and believable.
- **Summoner**- A psychic power that lets the user make contracts with pure faeries, letting the summoner call them in times of need. Each creature has an anchor, some item symbolizing the bond. Mastery of summoning takes decades of study, which is why the most powerful are either vampires or past middle age.
- **Seelie**- The Sidhe queen's court. The Seelie way is about following the letter of the law, even when it's hard or cruel. They have a hard time reconciling faerie rules with the new mortal laws since the Big Reveal.
- **Solar Magic**- The power to conjure, control, or banish sunlight. Some of the most powerful practitioners can find hidden objects or discover long-kept secrets.
- **Solar Affinity**- A trait some solar magi have that makes them beacons for coincidence.
- **Space magic**- The power to move the self or objects instantly across distances. Some can even move other people.
- **Space Affinity**- This space power comes with an ability to locate people or things important to the magus.
- **Telekinesis**- A psychic power that moves objects.
- **Telepathy**- A psychic power to read minds.
- **Tithe**- The process of pledging to either the queen or king, making a changeling choose to be either Seelie or Unseelie.
- **Umbral magic**- The power to conjure, control, and banish shadows and veil or camouflage objects or people.
- **Umbral Affinity**- A trait some umbral magi have that makes them difficult to remember without psychic ability, faerie magic, or a shifter pack bond.
- **Undeath magic**- The power to conjure, control, and banish unliving energy.

- **Unseelie-** The Goblin king's court. The Unseelies bend the rules and often navigate mortal society more easily than their Seelie counterparts.
- **Water magic-** The power to conjure, banish, and control water.
- **Wood magic-** The power to conjure, banish, and control wood. It takes extreme power to influencing a living plant.

Creatures

- **Basilisk-** A venomous serpent that also has poison magic.
- **Dragonet-** A tiny dragon-like creature, always associated with one or more element which powers their breath attacks later in life. They have scales but are warm-blooded like birds. Most don't get much bigger than a small cat.
- **Familiar-** A magical or mythical creature who makes a bond with a magus.
- **Gryphon-** A chimera which has the head of a bird and hindquarters of a predatory mammal. They come in several combinations of base species, and habitat influences their choice in magi to bond with.
- **Karkus-** A crab that can change its shape. They're said to be the offspring of the crab that pinched Hercules as he battled the Hydra.
- **Lightning Bird-** A familiar from South Africa with an affinity for lightning. Its beak can jump-start a car.
- **Mercat-** A shapeshifting feline with fur for land and scales in the water. They can live in lakes, rivers, or in the sea as well as on land. They must never completely dry out, or they will die.
- **Moon Hare-** A magical rabbit that gets power from its particular moon phase. They commonly bond with umbral magi.
- **Pharaoh's Rat-** These natural predators of dragon shifters are the size of ferrets and resemble a mongoose with more

fur. They have an affinity for space magic and can use it on occasion.

- **Pigeon**- Not as mundane as most think, some pigeons have an uncanny sense of direction due to their affinity for air magic.
- **Pricus**- An aquatic goat said to be descended from Capricorn. They can warp time even better than Gnomes.
- **Pure Faeries**- Creatures who spring to life from magical sources in the Under. They are genderless, and their type and ability depend on place of origin. They're associated with only one court, although they will work together to defeat a common enemy.
- **Sand Cat**- A feline that lives in the desert, able to go for weeks without water. Earth magic lets them do this.
- **Sha**- A magical desert dog from Egypt. Sha are the size of mundane toy breeds with short hair and small pointy ears. They could pass for mundane except for their blue tongues. They are attracted to anything undead.
- **Sphinx**- A magic cat with an affinity for fire. The reason they're hairless is that they're resistant to flames.
- **Strix**- A venomous owl with an affinity for poison. Female striges have rounded tufts on their heads, while males have pointed ones.
- **Sumxu**- A lop-eared cat found only in northern China. They are masters of camouflage and have an affinity for several kinds of magic.

Places

- **The Academy**—Something between a community college and a military academy for extrahumans, the Academy is geared toward helping extrahumans who don't play well with mortals get ready to join a blended society. It's got divisions for learners of all ages, though they are housed separately.

- **Cherry Blossom School**- A dojo geared toward teaching extrahumans self-restraint, meditation, and how to temper their enhanced physical abilities with more mundane skills. It's been around for close to a hundred years, run by the Ichiro family. Mundane classes used to be offered as a front but now are a separate division.
- **Ellicot City Magitechnic**- A prep school for magi and psychics specializing in magipsychic technology. It's located outside Baltimore.
- **Gallows Hill School**- Traditionally for shifters, this prep school in Salem recently opened its doors to changelings and other extrahumans not categorized as magi or psychics.
- **Hawthorn Academy**- A preparatory school for magi in Salem. Its campus is in the space between the mortal realm and the Under, giving it unrivaled privacy. They specialize in teaching familiar magic.
- **Providence Paranormal College**- A school founded just one year after Brown University and located right in its shadow. Providence Paranormal used to admit only magi and psychics, but it's been accepting all types of extrahumans ever since Henrietta Thurston became headmistress. There has been trouble since then for students and faculty, leading people to believe dissenters are sabotaging the school.
- **Trout Academy**- A prestigious preparatory school for changelings with magic, recently open to magi and magical shifters. Its campus is located in South County and has been operating in some form or another since Rhode Island Colony was founded.
- **The Under**- The faerie realm. It's been divided into two parts ever since the Sidhe Queen and the Goblin king split up thousands of years ago. Mortals don't age in the Under, but it's a dangerous place for them to be. Getting lost means never being seen again, and it's easy to get indebted to

something nasty while trying to get through or out of the
Under.

- **Wolf Messing Prep**- An institute for psychics to learn to
control their skills before heading to college.

Events

- **The Big Reveal**- The term used for the 1990s, when the
world discovered magic was real and extrahumans existed.
The decade was marked with fear as everyone adjusted to
the changes. Since the 21st Century, law and technology
work for both humans and extrahumans.
- **Boston Internment**- A reaction by Boston government
officials to the disappearance and suspected trafficking in
extrahumans, especially shifters. All registered extrahumans
in Boston lived on barges for close to a month under guard
by the Boston Police. The traffickers got their hands on
some magical gadgets, rendering the protection useless.
Few survived.

THANK YOU!

.

Thank you for reading! If you loved this book, please leave a review. You can find my other work by clicking the links below, going to **my website** or visiting my **Author Central page**.

ALSO BY D.R. PERRY

Providence Paranormal College

Bearly Awake (Book 1)

Fangs for the Memories (Book 2)

Of Wolf and Peace (Book 3)

Dragon My Heart Around (Book 4)

Djinn and Bear It (Book 5)

Roundtable Redcap (Book 6)

Better Off Undead (Book 7)

Ghost of a Chance (Book 8)

Nine Lives (Book 9)

Fan or Fan Knot (Book 10)

Hawthorn Academy

Familiar Strangers (Book 1)

Acting in Kindness (Book 2)

Fire of Justice (Book 3)

Learning to Give (Book 4)

Light of Equality (Book 5)

Worthy Lives (Book 6)

Mind of Distinction (book 7)

Gallows Hill Academy

Year One: Sorrow and Joy (Book one)

For other books by DR Perry please see her Amazon author page.

CONNECT WITH THE AUTHOR

Website: https://www.drperryauthor.com/

Join her newsletter!

Find more of D.R. Perry's books on Amazon.